Praise for Susan Hatler's Work

"Love at First Date left me completely satisfied."

— *Getting Your Read On*

"If you're looking for a fun, light read then look no further!"

— *Night Owl Reviews*

"I was laughing and smiling throughout the story."

— *Tifferz Book Review*

"Hats off to Susan Hatler for a five star book!"

— *Books Are Sanity!!!*

"Susan Hatler's books make me laugh out loud while also touching my heart."

— *Virna DePaul, New York Times Bestselling Author*

Titles by Susan Hatler

An Unexpected Date

Better Date than Never Series

Love at First Date (Book #1)

Truth or Date (Book #2)

My Last Blind Date (Book #3)

Save the Date (Book #4)

A Twist of Date (Book #5)

License to Date (Book #6)

Driven to Date (Book #7)

Up to Date (Book #8)

Teen Novels

Shaken

License to Date

(Better Date than Never #6)

Susan Hatler

Cover Design by Elaina Lee, For The Muse Designs
www.forthemusedesign.com

Chapter One

I shouldn't have sent out the wedding invitations. So obvious—*now*. The only upside? I'd chosen exquisite paper and Bickley Script font for the cancellation notices. Humiliating, but classy. According to my mother, good taste improved any situation. It was a motto she lived by, and I'd followed suit.

Always the good girl, that's me.

Unfortunately, the bridal boutique where I bought my wedding dress had a no returns policy. I'd chosen an off-the-shoulder chantilly lace trumpet gown that would never go out of style. Not that I'd ever wear it after what Paul DeWitt put me through. So I sold it online for a fifty-percent loss, which was a bummer.

Being married to a lying, cheating, slimeball would've bummed me out more, though.

Since my mom had raised me to control my emotions, I'd kept it together—at least on the outside. In private, I bawled my eyes out for two months straight.

Paul had called me for the first few weeks pleading with me to forgive him. He'd admitted cheating on me but said it had been *early* in our relationship. And if he had *known* she was my sister then he never would've dated her. Hard to believe he'd thought *that* apology would win me back. I'd grossly overestimated his intelligence.

That had been four months ago.

Now, I'd just closed escrow on a ranch-style house located on the Sacramento River—boo-ya! Unfortunately, my new home looked like the eighties had thrown up in it. The remodel overwhelmed me so I recruited my two girlfriends and we were currently peeling strips of orange rooster-covered wallpaper off my kitchen wall—a tedious task that was going three times faster than when I worked alone.

"My realtor asked me out," I announced, as I removed an impressively large strip of wallpaper (three roosters-worth).

Kristen let out a whistle as she defiled the poultry on the adjacent wall. "Guess he wanted more than a commission, huh?"

I wrinkled my nose. "Well, a commission is all he's getting. I turned him down."

"Is this the guy, Kaitlin?" Ginger gestured to the

calendar-magnet on my fridge, which included a glamour shot of my realtor, Chase McDermott. "Why would you say no to this fine specimen of a man? Just looking at him makes me want to buy real estate. Not that I can afford it."

"Oh, I hear you," I said, picking at a stubborn scrap of wallpaper that didn't want to come off. "If my dad hadn't given me the down payment, I'd still be renting, too."

Ginger rubbed her chin. "How'd you get your dad to pony up the cash?"

Shrugging, I said, "He offered, so I accepted. We don't really go into details about things in my family. It's all very polite and surface-like. But, I don't know, maybe he's trying to make up for divorcing my mom, moving to Seattle, and being absent most of my life."

"Darn." Ginger went back to scratching at her portion of wall. "My parents are still married so I'm out of luck."

I made a frowny face and pursed my lips. "Poor you."

"Back to Chase McDermott." Ginger gestured toward his picture. "H. O. T."

Kristen hummed her approval, too.

I flashed Ginger a wry smile. "Feel free to take down

his number and call him."

She twisted her long, dark hair around her finger, and seemed to think about it a moment. "He likes you, not me. It's been months since you dumped your loser ex. Time to get back in the saddle, girl."

I shook my head. "I'm not into horseback riding anymore."

Ginger huffed, then turned to Kristen. "You're a family therapist. Talk some sense into her."

Ugh. They were pushing me to date—*again.* My stomach knotted as I realized I'd brought this on myself by mentioning Chase. Not smart, Kaitlin. Not smart.

Kristen glanced my way, then surprised me by shrugging. "If Kaitlin doesn't want to date Chase McDermott, the most gorgeous man to walk the planet— after Ethan, of course—then that's her choice, and we should respect that."

Surprised, the knots in my belly loosened. "Thank you."

Kristen flicked a piece of paper off her sponge, then lifted her lashes. "Although it does seem like an awful waste. It's not like there's something horrifyingly wrong with him, right? He doesn't smell? Or pick his teeth with his fingernail?"

Ginger shuddered. "I hate when guys do that."

My mouth dropped open. "You were going to respect my decision, remember?"

Kristen shook her head. "I said we *should*. I never said we would. What gives, Kaitlin? Did you find out he has a rap sheet?"

I rolled my eyes. "Chase could be the most law-abiding citizen in Sac, I'd still rather spend my time doing something just for me—like remodeling my house. I'm using shabby chic beach-themed decor."

"Sounds gorgeous." Kristen scrubbed her sponge against the wall. "But can't you date him *and* decorate?"

I moaned. "Just drop it. I'm not interested in going out with Chase."

"You said the same thing when your mom wanted to fix you up with her friend's son, and you didn't have a good reason for turning him down, either." Ginger hopped onto my counter then leveled me with a stare. "Do you want to become a cat-lady, Kaitlin? Is that your goal?"

"Hmm . . . you could be onto something there. Felines are probably more loyal than a man. Thanks for the idea. Maybe I'll start with a calico—"

"You need to start dating," Ginger said firmly.

Kristen nodded. "It's really time."

I grunted and threw my hands up in frustration, my sponge flying through the air. It hit the floor, spattering water. "See what you made me do? I just want to fix up my house in peace, without you two ganging up on me."

Ginger pursed her lips. "Not gonna happen."

"As a successful woman in your late twenties, you're in your prime. You side-swiped being married to a two-timing cheat. You've earned a license to date. Take it, and drive." Kristen used an annoyingly reasonable tone. "Go out with a guy. Or two. Or five. Try men on and see how they fit. Don't think of it as stressful, more like window-shopping."

I leaned down, then nabbed my sponge off the floor. "Is this what therapy is like? Do you use these kinds of whacky analogies with your clients?"

"I don't have to because my clients listen to me." Kristen tilted her head. "At least, most of the time."

Ginger raised her hand. "If you start dating, I will help you paint the inside of your *entire* house."

I'd been heading to the sink to rinse my sponge, but

stopped short at this generous offer. "You do realize we're talking about two-thousand square feet?"

Kristen moved to stand next to Ginger. "We'll *both* help you."

A vision of my house entirely painted flashed through my mind—sandy-brown with white trim. While the thought of opening my heart to someone left a bad taste in my mouth, what would one drink with Chase hurt? "If I go on this date, you'd both have to help me from start to finish. Deal?"

"One date?" Ginger crossed her arms. "That's pacifying us, not getting back in the game."

The image of my beautifully painted interior evaporated and I panicked. "What's it going to take?"

Ginger turned to Kristen and they seemed to hold an entire conversation with their eyes and facial expressions, before finally nodding at each other.

"Five dates," Kristen said. "Then we'll stop worrying about you becoming a hermit and you'll have two slaves for your remodel."

"Five?" I groaned, then realized today was Saturday. If I went on five dates in five nights, we could start painting next weekend. "Not only would you have to stop bugging me about dating but you'd need to tell the girls at work to lay off, too. Because Ellen keeps trying to set me up with some guy from Henry's softball league."

"Agreed," they said in unison.

Ginger clapped her hands, then lifted my cell off the counter. "Call him. Now."

"You're relentless," I muttered, as she handed me the phone. "Fine."

Even though it was the last thing I wanted to do, I called Chase. We agreed to meet for a drink on Monday at the Geoffries hotel lounge—my idea since I'd attended New Year's at the Geoffries and my taste buds still remembered the deliciousness of their signature cocktail.

Five dates in five days. Then I could let my license to date expire and focus on making my home exactly how I wanted it. I'd arranged one date, four to go.

****

Sunday evening, I picked up my stepsister, Melanie, and we drove to Old Sacramento. Since I'd found out she'd been seeing my ex, things had been a little awkward between us. In her defense, she'd had no clue I'd been dating Paul, had been shocked when I'd introduced him as my fiancé, and hadn't known how to tell me the louse had been cheating on us (with each other). Probably would've been better if she hadn't confessed at my bachelorette party, though.

Just saying.

When Mel and I arrived in Old Sac, we still had a few minutes before meeting our parents (my mom, her dad) for dinner at The Boat House, so we slipped into a nearby boutique to browse the goodies they were selling.

I lifted a seashell-covered tissue-box cover from an antique shelf, trying to decide if I liked it. "Cute or tacky?"

"Either way, it'll be hard to dust." Mel pointed at the space between the shells. "Look at all those crevices."

That was Mel—ever practical. Even now she wore no make-up, had her blonde-hair thrown into a ponytail, and looked effortlessly gorgeous. I, on the other hand, had spent an hour applying makeup and taming my wild, red locks with a flat-iron. Unlike Mel, nothing came easily for me. Sigh.

I set the high-maintenance tissue-holder down, then examined a sea-foam blue vase. "I need a date. Know anyone single I could stand to be with for an hour?"

Mel turned toward me, her blonde hair bouncing over

her shoulder. "A whole hour? Gee, that sounds romantic."

Wrinkling my nose, I said, "I'm not looking for romance. I'm being *forced* to date. Kristen and Ginger have been hounding me for weeks, and yesterday I cracked. I need five dates in five days, then they'll help me paint the interior of my house."

"Kristen Moore?" Mel threw her head back and laughed. "Is a family counselor supposed to be pressuring you like that?"

"Right?" Turning the vase over, I checked the price and flinched. "Are you kidding me? It's made of glass, not gold."

"I love that." She gave an approving nod. "It would look great on that dark bookshelf in your living room."

I shook my head. "I've finally brought my savings to a comfortable level. I can't blow this much money on a vase—even if it was hand-blown in Italy and I'd have it forever . . . agh! Get me out of here before I break out my credit card."

Mel laughed, led me toward the door, then paused at a shelf filled with colorful candles. "Guess what?" She lifted a candle to her nose. "I have a job interview this week."

I sniffed the candle she held toward me. "For a teaching position?"

She nodded. "It's my third interview this summer so wish me luck that this school won't want someone more experienced, too. I'm existing on beans and rice right now."

Mel's hours as an aerobics instructor had been cut recently when new management had taken over the gym so I knew her budget was tight. Always looking on the bright side, she decided to finally use her major in early-childhood education to teach. "I'll be crossing my fingers for you, sweetie."

"Thanks." Mel laced her arm through mine, the bell chiming behind us as we strode out the door. "So, you need a date."

I stopped at the edge of the sidewalk. "A second one, actually. I've scheduled the first."

"Really?" Mel checked for cars before we crossed the cobblestone street, her ponytail bouncing over her shoulder. "With who?"

"My realtor." Fingering the edge of my silky hair, I couldn't help thinking how much time I'd save each morning if I just put my hair up the way Mel did. But my mother had taught me to always look my best, and casual didn't cut it in Mom's book. "I need four more dates for the deal, though. Mom tried to set me up a few weeks ago so I'm going to see if he's still available. His mother is Alisha Burnside from Mom's Spritzer Ladies golfing group."

Mel stopped before the double glass-door entrance of The Boathouse. "You know that ladies group is just their excuse to look respectable while drinking before noon."

I giggled, agreeing with her one-hundred percent. "Still, Alisha's son could be decent to hang with for one cocktail."

She held a finger in the air. "Apparently Janet failed to tell you she already tried to set *me* up with Brian Burnside."

My brows scrunched together. "Mom did that?"

Mel nodded. "Trust me, no potential there."

It's like she wasn't listening to me. "I don't need potential, just a second date."

Her eyes widened. "You're missing the point of why your friends set up this dating deal. Don't you want to find someone wonderful? Like Matt?"

Yeah, Mel's boyfriend was eighty shades of awesome. But guys like Matt were a rare breed. And it's not like I needed a man in my life to be happy. Besides, my remodel kept calling to me and all I could think about were two words: free labor.

I reached for the door. "What I want is to concentrate on my house, my *sanctuary*. I'm going to power through these dates so they don't slow me down from my real goal."

Mel leaned toward me as she breezed through the entryway, whispering, "Brian Burnside is also jobless."

My brows came together. "Really? Mom said he's an architect."

Not that it mattered.

Spotting my mother inside, I strode toward her with only one thing in mind: a date for Tuesday night. After Brian, I'd only have three more dates until I was home-free.

****

On Monday, Ginger spread the word to everyone at work about my date with Chase, and they were all making a *big* deal about it. As the human resources manager at Woodward Systems Corporation, I pulled rank and sent a mass-email reminding everyone that personal topics of conversation should not be discussed during work hours.

Then I ditched out of the office twenty minutes early.

Man, if one more person asked me if I was excited, I might scream . . . and confess that I was *only* dating under duress—not for the joy of it. As if. These dates were a means to an end. Nothing more.

Seriously, what was wrong with focusing on myself right now? My dad had moved away from me when I was twelve. My fiancé had cheated on me (with my sister, no less). What sane woman would be eager to go back for more?

Not *moi*.

My heels clicked across the marble lobby as I entered the Geoffries hotel, glancing at the small line at the check-in counter and then over at the concierge desk where the elderly concierge was helping a woman holding a sweater-wearing poodle. Hopefully he was informing this obvious out-of-towner that it was ninety-eight degrees outside so if her dog needed an outfit it should be a bikini for the pool.

I, myself, wore a short-sleeved silk wrap dress that

was warm enough for the office air-conditioning, but wouldn't make me fry (much) when I stepped outdoors into the oven we called Sacramento in August.

Turning toward the lounge, I strode past a gold-framed advertisement for the Geoffries' annual Black & White Ball, and another event called Descending for Diabetes. The Geoffries hosted the finest parties, housed luxurious suites, and served amazing drinks in their bar.

Only the latter interested me right now.

I entered the regal lounge, checking my watch. Over half-an-hour early for my date. Propping myself onto the navy-blue and gold patterned chair at the bar, I pulled out my cell to text Chase. If he was available now then we could start the date early and we could *end* it early. Brilliant idea.

"Would you like something to drink?" a smooth male voice asked.

The bartender appeared in my peripheral vision, but I kept my eyes fixed on my keypad as I ordered, "A Geoffries Martini, please?"

"Your wish is my command," he said, then stepped away.

If only he could actually grant wishes. Then maybe

I'd get free labor, no strings attached. A bartender-genie, that's what I needed. . . .

The bartender shook my drink, ice clinking around the shaker. "Waiting for friends?"

"No, I—" My mouth froze when my gaze connected with deep blue eyes that sent an electric jolt through me. Heat curled my toes and my mind went blank. "Um, what?"

The corner of his mouth lifted. "Just asked if you're meeting anyone."

"Yes, a date." I cleared my throat, trying not to focus on how the bartender's tousled dark hair made his sapphire-blue eyes stand out even more. After all, I couldn't invite him to be date number three now that I'd told him I was *on* a date. Or could I . . . ?

His brows came together as he poured pink liquid into a martini glass. "You don't sound too thrilled about your date. This a set up?"

"I'm looking forward to my date," I protested.

Not a lie. I was looking forward to having it, then having it be over.

"I don't buy it." He set the cocktail in front of me, then gave an inquisitive side-glance that turned my insides liquid. "You look more annoyed than excited. Why don't you tell me what this date is really about?"

Wrapping my fingers around my glass, I ignored the flutters in my belly, and the desire to tell him *everything*. "You don't want to hear about my problems. I'm sure you're super busy."

He leaned onto the bar, bringing those mesmerizing eyes level with mine. "Not terribly."

With him so close, I breathed in his musky scent and my heart jumped into my throat. "Are you this attentive to everyone you serve?"

His gaze left my eyes, trailing down to where my long red strands rested over my shoulder. "Only the beautiful redheads."

A burst of laughter escaped. "You did not just say that."

"Made you smile, didn't I?" The corner of his mouth turned up revealing an adorable dimple. "No, really. What's going on?"

My smile faded and the past four months came crashing back, ending with the deal I'd made. "Like I said, just waiting for my date."

As if I'd confide in a man I'd known all of two

minutes. Especially a guy with major charm and hypnotic blue eyes. Did he think I was that easy?

"Excuse me a moment." He tapped two fingers against the white granite countertop, then swiveled toward the other end of the bar to serve two women I hadn't seen sit down.

A sudden wave of disappointment crashed over me, which was ridiculous. I didn't want to chat with the bartender. I wanted my date to arrive and then leave so I could scratch one date off my check-list. I scanned my phone to see if Chase had gotten my message and could come early.

No incoming texts. Sigh.

With nothing else to do, my eyes drifted toward the bartender whose back was to me. No harm in stealing a quick peek as he mixed the ladies' drinks, right? Also no harm in admiring the way his white shirt stretched over broad shoulders, his black vest tapered down to a trim waist, and rested nicely over his snug-fitted pants.

The hot bartender clearly worked out.

Giggling erupted at the end of the bar and my eyes flicked to the two women, who fluttered their fingers at me. My gaze traveled to their faces and my jaw dropped open. "What the . . . ?"

It was Ginger and Kristen.

Chapter Two

My stomach tightened as Kristen and Ginger slipped onto the bar stools next to me. I rolled my eyes. "What are you guys doing here?"

"Reconnaissance." Kristen set her wine glass down on the counter, then swiveled toward me. "Making sure you don't renege on our dating deal."

Her loud voice practically echoed through the room and I glanced up to find the bartender smirking at me.

I downed the contents of my glass. "Get your paint brushes ready, ladies. After this stunt, you'll be working overtime."

"Maybe, maybe not." Ginger glanced around the lounge. "Where is Chase, anyway?"

"He'll be here." Not early, unfortunately.

Ginger rolled her long, dark hair around her finger. "We'll stick around to make sure you don't ditch out before he arrives. That pained look on your face doesn't exactly scream commitment, you know."

I pushed my empty glass away. "I'd be in less pain if you two weren't spying on me."

And if the bartender would stop shooting me smug looks. So I fibbed to a stranger about being excited about my date. Big whoop.

Kristen turned to Ginger. "We are being kind of overbearing. It's starting to remind me of my mother. We should give Kaitlin some space."

"Yes, please." I nodded, eagerly.

Ginger shrugged and stood. "Fine. We'll be right over there if you need us." She gestured toward a nearby cluster of elegant couches. "And remember, you might not want this date now but you'll thank us in a few years when you're popping out Chase's babies."

I threw my hands in the air. "That is so *not* going to happen."

"Keep an open mind. You never know." Kristen winked as she trailed after Ginger.

My jaw tightened and I was starting to rethink this dating deal. But scraping wallpaper and repainting would be so much work alone. . . .

"Another drink?" the bartender asked, his voice filled with humor.

A full glass appeared next to my empty one and I looked up gratefully. "Thanks. How'd you guess?"

"Long shot," he joked, then held his hand out. "Kaitlin, isn't it?"

"Yes." Refraining from tossing my friends a wicked glance, I found myself slipping my hand into his—tingles danced over my hand, up my arm, and my vision tilted. "And you are?"

His eyes dropped to our hands, making me wonder if he felt the same unbelievable sizzle of electricity. "I'm Paul."

My heart stopped and I scowled. I couldn't help it. The hot bartender might've been physically rocking my world, but he also shared the same name as my ex. I needed away from this bar. Fast.

He winced. "Uh oh. I can see the name has bad memories for you. Don't judge all Pauls by the same book."

When he squeezed my hand slightly, emphasizing his words, I couldn't let go. Or look away from those hypnotic blue eyes. . . .

Ping! Ping!

The chime from my cell broke whatever spell I'd been under and I managed to pull my hand away then run my finger across the screen. Chase! Thank goodness.

His text read: *Sorry, but I'm hung up with a client. Are you okay to wait a little bit? Should be done shortly.*

No, I was not all right to wait a bit. Not with Paul "the sequel" making my stomach do floppy things.

I typed back: *Yes, I can wait. See you soon.*

It's free labor, okay? Like fifty bucks an hour times two. I'd be crazy not to wait a little longer to save that kind of dough.

I lifted my lashes to find Paul "number two" peering down at me with an inquisitive expression. "My date's running late," I confessed.

"The date you're looking forward to?" His lips twitched as he picked up my empty glass and slipped it beneath the bar. "What *is* a dating deal, anyway?"

My cheeks heated. Oh the mortification. "Basically, my friends—the two over on the couch staring at us—are forcing me to date."

"Come on." He twisted a lime over a glass of water then pushed it toward me. "It's not like they can make you date."

"They *enticed* me into a dating deal, which is the same thing." Just like he was enticing me into telling him about my personal life. How did that happen? I normally excelled at refraining. Maybe I should wait for Chase in the lobby—away from this bartender's intoxicating charm. "Can I get the check please?"

"Hang on a sec." He stepped toward a couple who sat down at the bar.

As he moved away, every part of me wanted him to come back. Like *now*. A rush of anxiety shot through me and my nerves stood on red alert. These belly flutters needed to scram, so I could focus on making my home like the beach scene in my head—serene, comforting, and safe.

Provided I could afford it.

Under my friends' intense scrutiny, pressure to date "for real" pressed down on me like a ten-ton brick. Pressure to keep an open mind with Chase . . . or, whoever else I lined up to date. But the thought of being hurt again sparked a vise-like grip on my heart.

No, I didn't need a license to date. I needed a license to *decorate*. And my friends needed to go.

Whipping my fingers across my phone, I texted Ginger: *There are dozens of bars downtown. Pick another one to hang at. ANY other one. Pretty please?*

Turning my head, I watched Ginger pull out her cell,

scan the screen, then whisper to Kristen. Hopefully they were discussing an alternate location. I loved my friends, but it was ridiculous that they'd followed me here.

Ping! Ping!

Ginger replied: *We prefer watching you flirt with the hot bartender. What's his story? Single?*

With Paul's friendly personality (and his mega hotness), he had to have a girlfriend. Maybe several. I glanced over to where Paul *"part deux"* mixed the couple's drinks while making snappy conversation. No way he was single.

I tapped out my reply: *Don't know, and don't care. His name is PAUL. Need I say more?*

After a sip of my drink, my phone beeped, and I found a text from Kristen: *I'll caulk your tub if you get Paul's #.*

In an ultimate betrayal, my mouth watered at the offer: *You're bluffing. Marriage therapists don't know how to caulk anything.*

A few seconds later: *Ethan remodeled his entire house on his own. He'll help me.*

Smart thinking, using her boyfriend as a negotiation tool. Since it'd be nice to take a bath without worrying about water seeping into my wall, I sent: *You're on.*

Paul returned, slid my check over to me, then picked up our conversation as if he'd never left. "Dating deal or not, part of you must want to go out with this guy or you wouldn't be here."

"Not even one molecule," I assured him, then took a deep breath and blurted, "Can I get your phone number?"

He'd been running my credit card, but stopped to stare at me—his deep, blue eyes widening in surprise. He stared at me for a few seconds as if assessing me. Then his gaze wandered over to Ginger and Kristen, then back to me. For a moment, uncertainty and disappointment flashed in his expression. Abruptly, I realized that even hot, flirtatious bartenders had feelings and he clearly thought I was playing some game with him.

Feeling like I'd swallowed a rock, I said, "I'm sorry. Forget it."

He set my receipt and credit card in front of me. "Is this part of your dating deal?"

"No." My stomach roiled at the white lie and I felt compelled by honesty to say, "This was for a different deal and you must think I'm horrible. But we're just playing a silly game. I'm not making fun of you. I think you're great. I even think the guy I'm meeting tonight is nice. But I'm—I'm trying to take a break from dating and my friends have been pressuring me so . . ."

"So you've decided to turn the tables on them," he said with a slow smile.

Relieved that he was no longer looking at me like I was scum, I nodded.

His eyes softened. "Someone hurt you?"

I stiffened. "Pardon?"

"You said you wanted a break from dating. I assume it's because some guy hurt you."

Hurt me? More like ripped my heart out of my chest, smashed it against the dirty city sidewalk, then stomped on it for good measure. I shrugged. "That's life, right?"

"Not my life. And it shouldn't be yours, either."

I stared at him in shock. I just met this guy and he didn't know anything about me—

"Not that we know each other, of course," he said. "So I don't expect you to believe me." He winked. "I think you're doing the right thing by taking a break, though. If you're not ready to date, you're not ready. So what do you get if I give you my phone number? Because that's it, right? You weren't planning on actually asking me out?"

He watched me carefully. Looked almost as if he wanted me to correct him. But that couldn't be what he wanted. He was probably just being insightful. Bartenders were the world's best counselors, right? He could likely give Kristen a run for her money. Plus, working in a bar, this guy must meet women all the time. He was just good at the over-the-bar talk, and must not realize when he switched from friendly to flirty.

I shook my head. "Just need your phone number. If I get it, Kristen has to caulk my tub. I bought a house that I'm remodeling. If I go on five dates, they've agreed to help me paint the interior. I'm waiting for date number one."

"When are you planning to paint?"

"This weekend."

His eyebrows rose and he grinned. "Go you, spunky. That'll teach them to try and pressure you."

My mouth turned upward and I felt happier than I had in a long time. Of course, that immediately made me worry. I was done with relying on guys to make me happy. At least I thought I was. . . .

"So, how about it then?" I pushed the pen toward

him.

"Hang on a sec," he said, then scooted down the bar to wait on a middle-aged man.

My eyes immediately followed him until my cell pinged.

Did you get it? Ginger texted.

No.

Did you ask?

Yes. There. Let her feel bad that she'd encouraged me to ask for a hot guy's phone number and I'd gotten shot down. Maybe they'd feel so badly they'd actually leave before Chase got here. Or so I hoped.

"Is that them?"

My head jerked up. Paul squared (though nothing about this guy was square in any way, that's for sure) had returned.

"W-What?" I stammered.

He smiled, the corners of his eyes crinkling in the most adorable way. "Are your friends texting you about getting my phone number?"

"Yes," I said reluctantly, not wanting to lie to him but not wanting to say anything that would make my friends look bad in his eyes. Deep down, I knew they just wanted me to be happy.

"Want to have some fun at their expense?"

If I'd caught any sense of meanness in his tone, I would have shot him down, but he didn't seem to have a mean bone in his body. He was all easy-going charm and I reminded myself that Ginger and Kristen *had* followed me here. I caught the mischievous glint in his eyes and a fun little zing zipped through my body. "What do you have in mind?"

He leaned toward me, bracing his elbows on the table. In an instant, his amicable expression turned to one filled with heat. I sucked in a breath as he reached out and tucked a strand of my hair behind my ear. Then he leaned closer, making me shiver with every little puff of breath that tickled the sensitive skin on my neck.

I could practically hear Ginger and Kristen's shocked intakes of breath behind me.

"How's this for starters?" he whispered.

"Not bad," I said, trying not to hyperventilate. He smelled so good and all of a sudden I had the strong urge to pull him down and kiss him. Just plant my mouth on his, not caring who saw us. Not caring who I was supposed to be meeting or that I wasn't supposed to be dating for real.

But the new Paul was playing with me. He had to be. So I cleared my throat and decided to beat him at his own game. I wrapped my hand around his neck, turned my head until my lips just about touched his, then whispered, "Does this mean I get your number?"

He pulled slowly back. Straightened. Then shook his head. "Nope."

My eyes rounded in shock. "Nope?"

"I don't think your date would like it."

"But my date's not here and . . ."

"Kaitlin?" came a voice behind me.

I slowly turned on my seat. And saw Chase.

I was so busted.

Chapter Three

"Kaitlin Murray," I said, leaning toward the speaker phone on my desk at work.

"I have Kristen on the line for you. Again." William, our receptionist, called out in a strained voice. "She's not taking no for an answer."

This was the third time Kristen had called and I also had two voicemails from her on my cell. Hoping she hadn't given poor William an earful, I relented. "Okay, put her through."

I waited for the ring, then snatched up the receiver. "Save your breath. I don't want to talk about Chase, last night, or anything remotely related to dating. And, prepare yourself, because in four more days you'll be—"

"I'm engaged," Kristen said, but her voice lacked any trace of excitement.

My forehead creased as I leaned back in my office chair. "If this is some kind of trick you and Ginger have concocted, I don't get it."

"Well, get this: I. Am. Engaged."

My chest swelled. "Ethan proposed? When? I just left

you last night."

"This morning. We took his boat out for a quick run on the Delta to test out Ethan's new water ski. When I jumped in the water to cool off, he threw me a white life preserver with 'Will you marry me?' written around it in bright red letters."

Ethan had proposed on a life preserver? No wonder she didn't sound enthused. "Congratulations, sweetie. That's so . . . *creative* of him."

Kristen and Ethan had been history buddies before they gave into their feelings for each other and became a couple. I figured he would've proposed on an ancient scroll or something equally historical (and, um, boring). But a life preserver?

"It's an inside joke, but very sweet and thoughtful," she said, her tone softening a little.

"Well, as someone from the outside, I don't get it." I laughed. "But I'm really happy for you both."

"Thanks," she said, flatly.

"What else is going on, sweetie?" I checked my watch, then eyed the mound of paperwork in my in-box that I needed to plow through in the next hour before date number two. "Because you sound like someone torched your favorite history museum."

Kristen sighed. "It's my fault, really. In my rush of joy, I made the mistake of calling my mother with the good news. Now, she's making demands on where we get married—the Geoffries hotel, which, according to her, is the only suitable location in Sac—and their ballroom isn't available for eighteen months. So mark your calendar for a year from February. Apparently that's when I'll be getting married."

"That's ridiculous," I said, remembering how hard it had been to please everyone while planning my wedding with my ex.

"Yet what I have to do or I'll crush her wedding dreams for the only child she'll ever have—yes, she actually used that line on me. Nice, huh?"

Her mother knew how to give a guilt trip, that was for sure. "What does Ethan's mom say?"

"She's thrilled and thinks the Geoffries sounds *lovely*." Kristen sighed. "If she'd protested, even in the slightest, I would've had an excuse that my mom couldn't hold against me."

I shook my head, feeling bad that her engagement day had been deflated. "At least you're marrying the right person. That's huge. Don't forget I went through all the wedding prep drama for a fiancé who'd hooked up with the maid of honor."

"I'm sorry you had to go through that." Kristen moaned. "Maybe things will work out with Brian Burnside and you'll be planning your real wedding sooner than you think."

I rolled my eyes. "So not happening."

Then, for some strange reason, an image of Paul the bartender popped in my head. He was wearing a tuxedo, his blue eyes intent on mine, and his mouth curved upward as I walked toward him. . . .

The receiver slipped from my grasp and smacked against the desk with a *thwak*, and I hurried to pick it up and put it back to my ear.

"Kaitlin? You there?"

"Yes . . . just, uh, dropped the phone." The image of the hot bartender in his tux still burned in my mind and I started fanning myself. "Sweetie, I know it's easier said than done, but try to remember that this wedding is about you and Ethan."

"Tell that to my mom." She groaned. "My four o'clock is here so I have to go."

"No problem. Congrats again on your engagement!"

"Thanks and keep an open mind on your date tonight. You never know . . ."

"We'll see," I said, then hung up the phone, trying to delete the picture of Paul in his tux from my head.

Instead, it burned brighter and the corner of his mouth turned up in that cocky way of his as if to tell me he knew I wanted to erase him from my mind and he wasn't going anywhere.

****

"Chase thinks I'm a bimbo." It was a little past five o'clock as I leaned toward the mirror in my office, widening my eyes and applying black mascara to my lashes as I geared up for date number two.

"You? A bimbo?" Ginger yanked a tissue from the box and dabbed a small blob of black from my eyelid. "He does not."

"Oh, he does. And I don't blame him." My cheeks heated as I relived the feel of Paul's breath against my neck. "I kicked off our date by letting the bartender nuzzle my neck."

"Yeah, that was *hot*. We thought for a moment there you'd drop your date with Chase and go for the new

Paul." Ginger gave me an approving smile in the mirror then rolled her eyes when I frowned. "Oh, get over it. You're a single woman and he left you waiting at a bar. Not smart on his part."

"But that didn't mean I should let the bartender get fresh with me." Well, it had been an act but she didn't know that.

Fresh. That's what Paul the bartender reminded me of. A breath of fresh air that had made me feel alive. "Chase made a move on me outside the hotel after only one date. Bimbo. May as well tattoo it across my forehead."

Ginger thrust her hand on her hip. "Did you ever stop to think that maybe he just likes you? That he was trying to claim you before the bartender turned your head and stole you away?"

Too late for that. My head had certainly been turned and I hadn't been able to stop thinking of Paul. And now I was picturing him in a tuxedo? Crazy. Yet the image kept replaying in my head. . . .

"Hello? Kaitlin, are you there?"

I jerked from my thoughts and remembered Ginger's question. "Do I think Chase likes me that much? It's possible. Do I think he made the wrong move by trying to cop a feel on the sidewalk? Definitely."

She handed me my *Harlot Red* lipstick. Okay, it was called *Cherry Berry*, but they'd have to rename it after the way I'd behaved last night. "Kaitlin, to be fair to Chase, it was over with him before it even began. You weren't planning on going out with him again, right?"

I grimaced, guilty as charged. "Nope. And I'm not planning on going on another date with Brian Burnside, either."

Twisting a lock of dark hair around her finger, she eyed me in the mirror. "I think you're taking this whole dating deal in the wrong spirit. It's not meant to be a chore. We care about you. We just want you to get over Paul and start having fun again."

I had fun last night. With the new Paul. Ugh. I wanted to rip my hair out. Why couldn't I stop thinking about that bartender? He was such a flirt and I'd fallen for it hook, line, and sinker.

She squeezed my arm. "You seem upset. Maybe we should put a halt to this dating deal. If you don't want to go out with Brian—"

I shook my head. "No way. I *want* to go out with

him." And I did. Just like I'd go out with Ellen's husband's softball buddy tomorrow night. That left me with only two more dates to plan until she and Kristen would be at my command. "I'm getting these five dates done this week, so prepare yourself to paint my house this weekend." Yes, that's where I needed to focus my thoughts. Back on my house. Back on my new, beautiful start without having to worry about a man who was going to hurt me eventually.

My cell rang and I glanced at the screen. A call from my dad? Weird, I'd just talked to him a couple weeks ago when I'd closed escrow. We had a good relationship but didn't talk often, which could only mean he had a purpose. Since I didn't have time for a full conversation, I let it go to voicemail.

I put away my makeup, grabbed my sparkly wrap to wear over my silky black dress, then picked up the evening bag that matched my pink heels. "Well, I'm off."

She stepped back as I opened my office door. "Where are you and Brian meeting?"

"The Geoffries."

Ginger's eyes rounded. "Seriously?"

"I know what you're thinking, but it was Brian's

suggestion." It was also not my fault that during my date last night with Chase, the waitress had brought my drink and passed me a napkin with a note scribbled on it. *Sorry if I made things difficult for you. Come back tomorrow and I'll give you my phone number. Promise. Paul.*

That had been the most exciting part of the evening after Chase had arrived, even though I still couldn't understand why. Chase had been gorgeous and a decent date—even though the guy didn't know squat about texturizing a wall.

Mel had warned me about Brian Burnside and his lack of employment, but surely my mom knew otherwise since she always pressured me about nabbing a corporate guy who could "provide a good life" for me. Which, please, I could take care of myself.

But Brian Burnside should be good company for an evening. I'd find out at the Geoffries. Knowing how Paul was occupying my thoughts, I should have done the smart thing and made reservations somewhere else. Too late now, though, because Brian said he had something special planned there. Maybe a yummy dessert?

My stomach rumbled thinking about it.

I'd just have to avoid the bar, that was all. Should be

easy since I was meeting Brian directly in the restaurant. I gave him a quick text, confirming our plans. He texted back: *Sure. Looking forward to seeing you!*

****

While strolling several blocks to the Geoffries, I checked my voicemail: *Hi, Kaitlin. This is your dad. I'm going to be in Sacramento Friday for a business meeting. If it works for your schedule, I'd enjoy seeing your house before I fly out. Get back to me as soon as you've glanced at your calendar. Bye.*

Tension crept up my spine as I hung up the phone. Ever since Ginger had brought up my dad giving me the down payment for my house, niggling questions had lurked in the back of my brain. Why *didn't* my dad and I ever talk about anything deep? It's not like he was bossy or judgmental like my mom. I should've been able to tell him how abandoned I felt when he'd moved to Seattle. And how my break-up with my ex had devastated me. Pasting on a smile had always been my family dynamic, but I was starting to wonder if that was such a good thing. I mean, I'd started opening up to Paul so easily and I barely knew him.

Paul. Why was I thinking about him again?

When I arrived at the hotel, a mob of reporters greeted me outside the door and one shoved a microphone in my face. "Good evening, miss. Are you here to participate in Descending for Diabetes?"

"No," I said, remembering the advertisement in the lobby. Although I wondered what the event was about, I concentrated on squeezing past the reporters because I so didn't love being in the spotlight—poised in the background was much more my style "I'm, um, here for dinner."

Two doormen flanked the gold double doors and ushered me safely inside. I threw a grateful smile to each of them. "Thank you."

As I entered the lobby, I caught my breath. Once again, I admired the hotel's beauty. It was all polished marble and dark wood and subtle but classy décor. It was a premiere destination in Sacramento, but I'd never had to push through news personnel to get in before.

My heels clicked against the lobby floor and I knew there was going to be no getting around it. In order to get to the hotel's restaurant, I was going to have to go right past the bar. I wouldn't look for Paul, though. I'd keep my eyes straight ahead.

Right.

Who was I kidding? I wasn't going to be able to resist taking a peek. But that was okay. Not like I'd stop to chat. Or get his phone number. Although, if I did I'd get my tub caulked. . . .

Oh, man. What was wrong with me? I barely knew the guy. Maybe I was just fixating on him as a way to get over my ex-Paul (the cheating louse). But that was what my house remodel was supposed to be for. And unlike one flirty incident with a hot bartender, my cozy new house would be keeping me safe and warm for the foreseeable future.

As I strode past the bar, I casually turned my head . . . then frowned. There was a blonde female bartender serving tonight. No sign of Paul. Was he on a break? Or had he forgotten he had the night off when he'd written that little note on my napkin?

A rush of disappointment flooded me, but I tried to shake it off as I headed to the restaurant where I found Brian waiting for me.

He wasn't as handsome as Chase (or Paul), but he was cute in a sporty kind of way. Plus, according to my mom, he was an architect. And an architect should know a lot about renovating a house, so we could talk about a common interest during dinner. Maybe I'd learn some relevant info for my home.

"Hi, Brian." I held my hand out as I stopped in front of him. "So nice to finally meet you."

He smiled in a way that wasn't exactly revolting and might even be construed as cute. If I were into dating for real, which I wasn't. "Great to meet you, too," he said, giving me a gentle hand shake. "How's your mother doing?"

"She's wonderful, thanks." I shot one last glance behind me. Still only the blonde bartender. Whatever. I forced the corners of my mouth upward. "Have you been waiting long?"

He pressed his hands together. "Actually, I arrived a little early as part of the surprise."

I blinked. "Okay, I have no idea what you mean by that. Aren't we having dinner?"

"We are having dinner *after*." He wiggled his brows, then turned his head away and put his hand to the side of his mouth. "My date is here now."

I flinched at the loudness of his voice.

The dark-haired hostess walked up and gave us a

lovely smile. "Would you like to have drinks before you get started?"

I looked from the hostess to Brian. "Before we get started with what?"

"Yes, we definitely need a drink first." He gave me a mischievous look and started to follow her. Then he stopped when he realized I wasn't behind him. He spread his hands wide. "Trust me, you're going to love this."

Trust him? I didn't even *know* him.

"Actually, I don't love surprises." I tightened my wrap around my shoulders, finding it difficult to keep my composure. "Would you please tell me what we're doing?"

If his plans were short, I might be able to get some wallpaper peeling in tonight.

"Okay, I'll spill the beans." His face lit up, like he'd just won the California lottery, then he raised his arms and made gestures as if he were climbing a rope. "We're going to rappel down the Geoffries hotel."

I burst out laughing. "I'm sorry. It sounded like you said we're rappelling down the hotel."

He nodded enthusiastically. "That's right."

My mouth froze. "You're not kidding?"

He shook his head. "The Descending for Diabetes event costs a grand per ticket and I won two tickets on the radio. We're going to rappel down from the swimming pool terrace, which is on the fifth floor. Isn't that incredible?"

"Yes," I said, finding it incredible that he thought I'd rappel down the side of a freaking building. Staying calm, I glanced down at my silky dress, then held my finger up. "Let me just run home and change into my mountain climbing gear."

I was so *not* coming back.

Chapter Four

"Whoa." Brian reached out and grabbed hold of my arm before I could head toward the lobby (and out the door). "Don't worry about what you're wearing, Kaitlin. That's part of the fun of this Descending for Diabetes event. Everyone rappels down the building in their evening wear."

Making a mental note to never let my mom set me up again, I eased out of his grip. "No way, Brian. Everyone would be able to see up my dress. You should've told me to wear pants."

He shook his head. "They said the harness keeps everything covered."

The hostess reappeared—apparently having realized we hadn't followed her—and gave us a questioning look. "Do you prefer to have your drinks on the event terrace?"

A drink sounded *so* good right now. Maybe two drinks. Maybe if I had enough drinks they wouldn't allow me to go down at all. Hmm.

"Yes, the terrace might work better since we're getting pressed for time." Brian checked his watch, slipped his arm around me, then started forward toward the elevator.

"Brian," I said, surprised to find my legs moving along beside him. "I can't do this."

"Why not?" His brows came together as he punched the elevator button and gave an exaggerated sigh. "I've already given the radio show hosts our names and they're interviewing us shortly. It's for charity, Kaitlin. Your mom told me your cousin has diabetes."

Oh, way to lay on the guilt. "I give money every year, but—"

"Your mom also told me you were outdoorsy and adventurous." The elevator arrived and he motioned me in.

"Really?" I sighed, knowing my mother would say anything to marry me into her country club. She would so *not* approve of a charming bartender. Shaking my head clear of Paul—who I shouldn't even be thinking about since he hadn't followed through on his napkin promise (and because I was on a date with another man)—I cleared my throat, then stepped inside the elevator. "How does the charity benefit if I work up the guts to do this?"

He hit the button for the fifth floor. "Each participant,

or ticket, costs a grand which is donated to diabetes research. The Geoffries hotel matches every participant's donation once they've rappelled down the building."

"That's very generous of the Geoffries." In addition to fabulous drinks and hot bartenders (ugh, Paul on the brain again), the hotel also seemed to have a heart. Now I just needed to muster the courage to do this.

We arrived to the fifth floor and the elevator doors opened with a *ding*.

Brian held his arm out. "Ladies first."

"Thank you." I smiled politely—to mask the terror I felt inside—then stepped out onto the terrace, which was buzzing with waiters, music, and elegantly dressed guests. I might've been able to enjoy the festive outdoor atmosphere if I didn't know it was only our jumping off point. Literally. "So my mother told me you're an architect," I said, needing a distraction.

He slipped his arm around my waist and led me toward the bar. "That's right. I'm doing independent contracting right now, but I used to work for—"

"May I get you a drink?" A man asked from behind me.

I stiffened. That voice. I knew that voice. That husky,

manly, and yes, sexy voice. I'd dreamt about that voice last night. . . .

Sure enough, when I turned around, my eyes connected with Paul's sapphire blues. A jolt of electricity zapped through me. "You're here."

"I told you I would be." He smiled, the corners of his eyes crinkling. "Shall I give you my phone number now or later?"

Beside me, Brian stiffened.

So much for losing my floozy rep.

My cheeks heated. "I, er . . ."

Brian squeezed my waist, then he turned to me accusingly. "Do you know this guy, Kaitlin? Why is he offering you his phone number?"

"Brian, this is Paul." I stepped out of my date's grasp and gestured toward Paul who looked drool-worthy in a black and white tuxedo. Huh. The other waiters were in vests. . . Paul must be the head waiter tonight or something. "My friends asked me to get his number, actually. He's helping out with a . . . tub caulking project."

Brian's scowl immediately dissipated, and he thrust his hand out. "Nice to meet you, Paul. I'm an architect and work with a lot of contractors. I'd be happy to give your number out if you're looking for work."

Paul shook his hand then eyed him as if sizing him up. "Nice of you to offer, but I'm only doing this project as a favor for Kaitlin. Not looking for anything else."

Brian's brows drew together as if he were insulted that his offer had been declined. "My firm designed this hotel, as a matter of fact."

Uh, okay. Where had that come from? And hadn't he just said he was an independent contractor?

Paul's eyes narrowed, then they flicked to me. "Geoffries Martini for you, Kaitlin?"

A rush of pleasure vibrated through me that he remembered my favorite drink. "Yes, that sounds perfect."

"I'll take a dirty martini." Brian's voice rose a bit too loud for a drink order.

Paul's mouth formed a straight line. "Coming right up."

Instead of dashing off, Paul scribbled on a napkin, handed it to me, then smiled at me in a way that had my stomach doing flip-flops.

"Thanks." I watched him walk away, then glanced

down at the square paper napkin in my hand. Ten digits guaranteeing my bathtub a little TLC from Kristen (or her boyfriend, depending on how she worked it). My brows drew together at the unfamiliar area code. Not Sacramento, so I wondered where he was from.

"Kaitlin?"

My head jerked up at Brian's voice. "Huh?"

"I said it's time for our interview."

"But our drinks . . ."

He slipped his arm around me, leading me in the opposite direction where Paul had gone. "I'm sure the waiter can find us."

I bit my lip, hoping that was true.

****

During our interview with the radio talk show hosts, I let Brian do most of the talking, which seemed to suit him fine. He'd spoken at length about his independent contracting business but no word on his firm or how they'd designed this hotel. Weird.

When it was my turn, I kept my sentences short and sweet, thanking the Geoffries and the other sponsors for their hefty donations toward diabetes research and finding a cure. Then I gave a shout-out of love to my cousin and all those who suffer from diabetes.

While we were suiting up to rappel down the hotel—hard to believe I was really doing this—and being given instructions, camera flashes went off. I could only hope the pictures would be burned (or deleted, as the digital case may be) since my silky black dress was folded around me like a diaper under my harness. A photo I wanted frozen forever? Not so much.

As Brian scooted off to find a glass of water, I wandered to the edge of the terrace and watched the last of the sun go down. Tightening my wrap around myself, I inhaled, then peeked over the wrought-iron railing. The steep drop made my stomach lurch. A gasp escaped. Squeezing my eyes shut, I covered my heart with my hand.

Was I really going to jump off a freaking skyscraper in downtown Sacramento? Okay, we were only on the fifth floor, but how dire was the situation for me to say *only* the fifth floor?

My chest flickered with fear, but at the same time another part of me fluttered with excitement. I was so tired of being the safe good girl. Where had that gotten me, really? Single at twenty-eight, dating for a free paint job, that's where.

For once in my life, I wanted to take a chance. Do something risky.

"There you are." Brian's voice invaded my thoughts. "I was looking all over for you."

"You found me." I peered over the railing again, chills prickling across my chest. "I don't know how I'm going to do this, Brian."

He held his arms out while the extreme sports person adjusted his harness. "What's the big deal? We're attached to a rope."

Turning away from my (very unempathetic) date, who was being carted off for a reason I couldn't hear and didn't care about, I gripped the rail and looked down again. The people walking on the garden terrace below looked so small from this high up. A cold chill trickled down my spine.

Suddenly, I felt someone come up beside me. "Having second thoughts?"

Upon hearing that husky, sexy voice, my skin immediately warmed.

Lifting my lashes, I peered up at Paul. "No. I haven't gotten past my first thought, which is that I'm about to become pavement splatter."

He chuckled. "That would be some bad publicity for the hotel. You think we'd risk that?"

Okay, probably not. "Accidents do happen."

His electric blue eyes peered into mine. "But you want to do it. Don't you?"

My mouth dropped open. "Have you not heard a word I said?"

"I hear everything you say." He turned so his body was facing me. "I also see what you're not saying. You want to do this, but you're scared. Scared you'll get hurt."

Suddenly I wondered if we were talking about rappelling down a building or asking him on a date—a real one. I wasn't sure which option scared me more.

The second one. Definitely.

My shoulders raised as I looked up at him. "I'm not the kind of girl who rappels down buildings."

The wind blew a few strands of my hair across my face and he reached out and tucked them behind my ear, his eyes holding mine the entire time. "You're whatever kind of girl you want to be."

Yeah, he could say that because he'd never met my

mom. She'd raised me to be poised and proper twenty-four seven, marry a financially successful man—I'd slightly botched that one—join a country club, pop out two children, and never let anyone see me sweat.

None of her plans included rappelling down a skyscraper in downtown Sac. Although she had told Brian I was adventurous. Maybe she figured, at this point in my life, I was *that* desperate. As if.

Paul tucked another stray strand behind my ear. "What's going through that pretty head of yours?"

"Rappelling." Living. Taking chances.

The entire thought sounded crazy, totally dangerous, and actually kind of . . . exciting.

My insides warmed and energy pulsed through me. Suddenly, the chatter in the background disappeared and there was just Paul and me, standing on the dark-lit terrace high above the city and staring into each other's eyes. . . waiting. Waiting for me to decide what my life was going to be.

My lashes lifted to where his blue eyes were studying me. I swallowed, building up the nerve to say the words. "I want to jump," I whispered, when I really should have said I wanted to jump with him, not Brian.

The corners of his mouth turned upward. "Then what are you waiting for?"

With the decision made, my mouth spread into a smile and I shrugged. "Hook me up."

****

"Who's in charge of lowering the rope again?" I said, figuring it would be nice to say hello to the person who would (hopefully) keep me from plummeting to my death.

"Tony and I will be taking care of you," the extreme sports guy named Dave said. "We'll control your speed from that rig over there."

I stared at the giant metal spool of rope he'd pointed to, which had a crank on the side. "I won't be controlling my own pace?"

"Not at this event." Dave reached into his pocket, pulled out a card, then held it out. "But if you'd like to give it another go a different time then we can hook you up with that."

"Thanks." I accepted the card, but didn't exactly have any pockets in my harness or silky tank dress (they were holding my purse and wrap for safekeeping). When I saw Dave look over his shoulder at his co-worker, I glanced around to make sure nobody was watching then slipped the card into my bra just as Dave turned back around. My cheeks heated. "Uh, how will you be lowering us?"

"We'll clamp your rope onto this metal hook here." He touched the metal piece on my harness located just under my chest. "I'll be talking to you through your earpiece and Tony will be lowering you both at a slow but steady pace."

I nodded. "Slow and steady. I like the sound of that."

"No big deal." Brian came up and stood beside me with his legs spread wide. "Don't feel like you have to go easy on us."

"Speak for yourself." I tossed my date an annoyed look. Five floors and date number two would be over. Forget dinner, I was so ready to be done with him.

"Don't worry. You're not the first person to go down today. We've had over a hundred participants." Dave gestured toward the edge of the terrace. "Go ahead and stand on the platform."

I wondered if Paul had rappelled down the building. Probably not since it cost a thousand dollars to participate and I couldn't imagine a bartender's salary afforded that kind of luxury. Plus, he might have been working all day.

Although, I didn't know when his shift had started or when it ended either for that matter. My eyes flicked to where he was talking to some of the hotel staff. They were watching him with attention so he *must* be the head bartender tonight or at least in charge of the event.

Brian and I stepped onto the platform, and he put his arm around me. I suppose this was technically a date, but I didn't feel even remotely attracted to him and the feel of his arm made me cringe. Then I thought of Kristen's advice that I give him a chance. I was about to jump off a perfectly good platform, after all. I supposed I could give my date one more chance.

"What the . . ." Brian's voice trailed off as he looked below us, then he suddenly gasped. "This is insane."

"Are you okay?" My eyes widened as I watched him grip the railing then lower himself down on his knees.

Beneath his white knuckled grasp, his eyes were wide with terror. "Can we lower ourselves in the platform? We don't h-have to go down with j-just a rope, do we?"

Wasn't that the whole part of rappelling? "You said earlier it was no big deal."

Oh, sure. Now he gets all freaky about the drop. Where were his sympathies when I'd looked off the terrace?

I clicked my earpiece on. "Dave? Are you there, Dave? We have a situation."

Dave must not have turned on his headset yet, because he continued talking to Tony but Paul caught my eye and strode over immediately. "Are you all right?"

"Me? I'm fine." The intensity of his look made my heart skip. "But I'm not so sure about Brian."

A look of relief crossed his face, then he stared down at my date, who was crawling across the platform and onto the terrace. Instead of helping Brian, Paul raised his arm and a woman in an evening gown hurried over.

My jaw nearly dropped as she strode toward us with strong meaningful steps. Besides being gorgeous, she didn't look nervous at all. She'd probably rappel off the top of the building without a second thought. Fingers of jealousy crawled through me. Was she Paul's co-worker? Or were they more? Why else would she be looking at him so intently?

"May I help you with something?"

"Yes. Would you mind getting Dave? Mr. Burnside seems to be having second thoughts."

I opened my mouth to ask Paul how he knew Brian's

last name, but then shock rolled through me as I realized what Brian's second thoughts meant . . . I'd be rappelling down the building by myself!

I hurried over to Brian and knelt. "You can't desert me, Brian. I need to do this."

He looked queasy. "Not happening."

"What about what you said to me earlier? About it being no big deal? That we're attached to rope and all that garbage?"

He held his arm up in a weak gesture. "Can you not talk to me right now? I'm trying to keep my lunch from coming back up . . ."

I stood and marched back to the platform—alone. I was doing this freaking thing. For my cousin. For everyone with diabetes. For *me*, too. I scanned around for Paul but he'd disappeared. Disappointment flooded through me. It's not like Paul owed me anything, but I really thought he'd wish me luck. He was at work, though. Maybe they needed him at the bar or in the restaurant. Still, he could've at least said good-bye.

This was exactly why I was sticking to my home remodel. Men just disappointed me and—

"You ready to go?" Paul's husky voice came from

behind me.

Surprised, I swiveled around and faced him. He'd ditched his tuxedo jacket and tie, and was wearing the same black harness I had on.

My mouth dropped open. "You're . . . descending with me? Why?"

The corners of his eyes crinkled as he smiled. "To keep you company. You didn't want to go it alone, did you?"

"Not in the slightest." I let out a tentative laugh. "But, you're working. Is it all right for you to do this? I don't want you to get in trouble for me . . ."

"Don't worry." He winked. "I cleared it with the boss."

The beautiful woman returned. "You're not rappelling are you, Paul? I thought you—"

"Alice, can you get Dave's attention for me? We're ready to go."

The woman looked baffled. Like she didn't know how to respond. "Yes, of course."

I leaned toward Paul. "What was that about? I'm not causing a problem for you, am I? Tell me if I am because—"

"I promise, it's fine." His fingers began firmly tracing the harness at my shoulders, then he followed the nylon strap down over my chest—gulp!—and across my waist, then he pulled at the clip in front as if to make sure it was secured tightly.

"Dave already checked me." My body tingled at every place his hands had run and I so wanted to check *his* harness. "You didn't have to do that."

He brushed both sides of my hair back from my face, secured it with a ponytail holder he'd seemed to pull out of nowhere, then left his arms around me as he leaned forward. "Yes, I did."

"You ready, Paul?" Dave appeared, then turned Paul away from me to check his harness as he spoke. "Your friend tossed his cookies by the plant inside the door. I called housekeeping."

"Kaitlin's friend, not mine."

Loved how quickly he pointed that out. "He's more of an acquaintance, actually."

Paul raised his brows. "Date number two?"

"It was for the remodel," I reminded him, then held my arms up as Dave triple-checked my harness—which wasn't nearly as enticing as when Paul had done it.

"You guys are all set." Dave clipped the ropes onto our harnesses, double-checked them, then gestured to his co-worker giving him the thumbs-up sign. He handed Paul an earpiece. "Facing the platform, you're going to climb down the three steps, then ease off and the rope will hold you. Remember, straight legs are strong legs so just lean back and walk your way down the building. We'll lower the rope slowly, so you'll have time to enjoy the view. Give us a shout in the earpiece if you want us to increase or decrease the speed. Sound good?"

"Yes," Paul said.

I swallowed when Dave turned to me. "Yes."

"Who wants to go first?" Dave looked at each of us.

Paul turned to me. "You have a preference?"

"Second," I said, without hesitation.

With one last tug on my rope, Paul moved to the staircase. Dave tested the sound in our earpieces once more, then with a final smirk Paul descended, and disappeared from sight.

My heart dropped and I scooted to the edge, holding my breath as I peered over while trying not to look *all* the way down. "Paul?"

My voice came out louder than anticipated and

could've been considered strained. With the platform in the way, I couldn't see him. What if he'd fallen? Pulse pounding, I started to panic. . . .

"I'm here, Kaitlin." His voice was calm and quiet, which soothed me immensely. "Your turn."

"Don't look down," I reminded myself as I dangled my first leg over the edge until it rested firmly on the step below me. Three steps. Dave had said there were three steps.

My top teeth ground against my bottom lip as I lowered my right foot to the second step. My legs were shaky and I knew I was crazy for doing this. Freaking Ginger and Kristen, and their dating deal. Still, at the same time, that tingle of excitement bubbled up and I only hoped it wouldn't be the end of me.

Somehow my left foot found the third step and I braced myself knowing there weren't anymore beneath.

"Looking good." Paul's voice came through my earpiece and I had to remind myself that he was right below me even though I couldn't see him because I refused to look down. "Ease your right foot to the bottom step then bend your knees to lower yourself."

I did as instructed, my death-grip tight on the hand

rail as I sat hunched on the last stair.

"Good. Now ease your legs off, then once you feel comfortable, let go."

"Really, Paul? Who is *comfortable* hanging off the side of a skyscraper?" I said, then heard him chuckle in response.

I'd never been so freaked out in my life.

Or as exhilarated.

I was five freaking floors above the earth. Then I'd let go and there'd be nothing holding me to the building except for a yellow rope that, I'm sorry, didn't look all *that* much thicker than a shoestring.

Pretending I was easing into a pool, I lowered my legs . . . then became very aware there was no water to hold me up. My feet dangled in the air and a breeze blew by, tickling my feet through my strappy heels, and reminding me there was nothing below me.

With one last look at the rope clipped to my chest, my hands tightened at the spot right above the bottom of the hand rail and I closed my eyes. "Paul?"

"I'm here, Kaitlin. I won't let anything bad happen to you. I promise."

Hearing his voice and, oddly enough, believing him, I let go.

Chapter Five

I dangled in the air, high above the city, scared out of my mind as to what would happen next. In those few seconds, with my life out of my own hands, panic filled every pore of my body—until a warm hand gripped my own.

At the same time that my heels connected with the side of the building, my gaze flashed right, and beautiful blue eyes greeted me.

Paul's mouth turned upward. "Fancy running into you here."

Warmth flowed through me momentarily, then terror fought its way back up. "Please tell me you've done this before."

"Don't worry. You're in good hands." He squeezed my hand as if to emphasize it. "How do you feel?"

I gulped. "Like I'm standing against the side of a building on shoes that are way cuter than they are comfortable."

His eyes traveled down the length of my body, a trail of heat following his path. "Sometimes you have to ditch comfort to live the life you want."

Looking into his eyes, I couldn't help wondering if he was talking about me or himself. "You think I want a life with pretty shoes?"

"Well, obviously." He glanced down at my strappy heels again. "Among other things . . ."

Butterflies fluttered in my belly and I had to remind myself there wasn't a safety cable to save me from *him*. If my investment counselor ex could cheat, what were the odds that a charming bartender would when he had scores of women available to him?

Remodel. Must focus on the remodel. "The lengths I'll go to for free house painting."

He chuckled, then gave instructions to Dave to start lowering us. As Paul's long, muscular legs stepped backward, he turned back to me. "Besides painting the interior, any other house projects you're working on?"

"Hmm . . . where to start?" I jerked unexpectedly when my rope started moving and Paul's thumb rubbed across the top of my hand. The feel of his skin against mine felt way too good, and immediately alarmed me. So I eased out of his grasp and focused on putting one foot behind the other as the rope lengthened at a steady rate.

"One of my favorite things about my house is that it's on the Sacramento River. There are steps at the end of the backyard that lead down to my own dock."

His brows furrowed quizzically. "Do you have a boat?"

Steadying my pace down the side of the building, I shook my head. "I don't have a boat, but I love being near the water ever since . . . well, I just love being by the water."

Paul opened his mouth—

"The previous homeowners left a faded red wooden table with chairs by the dock," I quickly went on. "I bring a glass of wine down every evening to relax. Well, not this week since I'm, you know, rappelling down a building and all."

The corner of his mouth turned up and we exchanged a look that warmed my belly.

I cleared my throat. "There's a great space by the dock. When I can afford to, I'll tile the entire area. First, I'm going to sand the paint off the table and chairs, then stain the wood deep blue like the ocean."

And Paul's eyes. . . .

He smiled, seeming to enjoy my rattling. "You're

very ambitious."

"It's a great set. Just needs a little TLC." Picturing what my home would look like after I'd finished gave me a serene feeling—that same feeling I'd had that week we'd spent by the beach in Kauai, right before my parents had split. "The entire house is a major eighties remodel, but I like replacing the old with my style. Makes the home mine."

His eyes sparkled as if he got what I was saying.

While leaning back, I concentrated on putting one pink heel behind the other. "It's not like I wouldn't enjoy some help, though—which, I'll have this weekend from Ginger and Kristen. Well, if Kristen's up for it, that is."

He rubbed his knuckle across his chin. "Isn't her help part of your dating deal?"

Thinking back to her phone call, I said, "Yeah, but she and her boyfriend just got engaged and her mom gives the word 'overbearing' new meaning. She's insisting Kristen and Ethan get married at the Geoffries hotel, but the earliest they could book is eighteen months from now."

His brows came together. "What's Kristen's last name?"

"Moore." I glanced over at him, wondering why he'd ask that. "You met her last night. She was wearing the white, button-up blouse."

"I remember her." He nodded, seeming deep in thought.

As the silence drew on, I started to feel uncomfortable. Why had I told him so much about me? And why did I want to tell him more? The pull I felt toward him unnerved me.

Needing a distraction, I glanced up to see the distance we'd covered and it was about one story's worth. Amazing that we'd gotten this far and I hadn't needed a sedative. I turned back to Paul who I found watching me intently with those amazing eyes. "Do you own your own house?" I asked, having no clue what a bartender's salary was.

There was an awkward pause, then he finally said, "I'm new to the area, so I'm staying here."

My forehead crinkled, remembering his out of town area code. "You're living at the hotel?"

"For now." He eased down the building next to me and I tried not to stare at the muscular shape of his legs. "If you're interested, we just replaced the patio tiles in the garden terrace and we have a lot of leftover tiles. They're Mediterranean style. Easy to install, too . . . there's a video online that gives a step-by-step. If you'd like, I can take a look at your space and see if the tiles would work there."

Wow. Someone willing to help me with my remodel without strings attached . . . that was something new. "That's really nice of you, Paul. Thanks."

"No problem. I'll show you the tiles when we get down."

When we get down? Laughter bubbled up inside me. I'd forgotten how high we were. Lost in my conversation with Paul, it felt like we were strolling (backwards) down a mountain or something. It was hard to believe I'd been worried. . . .

Then I glanced beneath me.

Nothing.

My stomach dropped and my feet halted as I gaped at the darkness spread out below. The dotted city lights blurred. "Oh . . . my . . ."

"Kaitlin? Don't look down. Look at me." Paul's voice was low, calm, and commanding. "Right here, Kaitlin. Lift your eyes."

I wanted to look over at him. I really did. But the horror had grabbed me with its claws, holding me captive, and I couldn't tear my eyes away from the vast empty space below.

My knees shook as terror sliced through me. Somewhere in the back of my mind, I realized the rope had stopped moving and I was vaguely aware of voices in my earpiece. I even felt hands grip my waist, but I couldn't tear my eyes away. Couldn't stop picturing myself spiraling down to my death.

"I c-can't—"

Suddenly, my view was blocked and warm lips covered mine—the terror inside me immediately ceased. What the . . . ? I couldn't speak. Couldn't think. With Paul's mouth capturing mine, I'd been thrust into a different kind of spiraling. One where my heart thudded, not in panic of dying, but from the amazing warmth flowing through me.

I wanted more. . . .

My mouth opened and Paul's tongue connected with mine. Chills vibrated down my neck and flutters danced through my belly as we searched, explored, and savored each other. I slid my fingers into that thick tousled hair, pulling him closer. His arms slipped around me, his fingers kneading into my back, and then I felt something rub insistently against my cheek—tugging me out of the heavenly fog I'd been in.

My eyes burst open and I saw the yellow rope nudging against me, reminding me of danger—only not from falling to the pavement below.

I pulled away from Paul abruptly, and he studied me through heavy-lidded eyes.

My heart pounded and my eyes widened. "Why did you do that?"

"To distract you." Cupping my face, his thumbs brushed my cheeks, then he leaned his forehead against mine. "Did it work?"

"Yes," I said, savoring the feel of his skin against mine.

Only now I was scared for a whole different reason.

****

Later that night, my doorbell rang, and I trudged to the front door in my painting sweats. In the twenty minutes I'd been home, I'd already touched up the white paint on my bathroom cabinets. The whole time I'd been painting, Paul's kiss kept replaying in my mind.

Not good.

Blocking the kiss from my head, I opened the door to find my sister on my front porch. "Mel! What are you doing here?"

She stepped inside, kicked the door shut behind her, and thrust her cell phone screen in my face. "Is this *really* you?"

"Is what really me?" I snatched the phone and stared at the image on the screen. There it was in color. Me. Paul. Attached to the side of the Geoffries hotel. Kissing. The caption under the photo read *Radio Love*. I gasped. "What the . . . ?"

Mel grabbed the phone back, tapped something on the screen, then started reading. "Brian Burnside and Kaitlin Murray find love thanks to local Sacramento radio station. It all began for the couple when Mr. Burnside won Descending for Diabetes tickets from—"

"Stop!" I pressed my hands to my ears, dropped down onto my living room sofa, and groaned. "How could this happen to me?"

"Seriously." Mel sat next me, staring at the picture on her phone. "So not like you to spider down a building and I really didn't picture Brian Burnside as your type. Is he a good kisser at least?"

Remembering the feel of Paul's lips on mine ignited a fire in my belly. "I did *not* kiss Brian Burnside."

Mel glanced from the picture to me. "Um . . ."

"The guy in the photo is the bartender from the Geoffries hotel. I can't believe our kiss is on the Internet." I buried my face in my hands. "I'm so mortified."

"And I'm so confused."

I straightened my spine. "Brian won tickets to rappel down the Geoffries hotel but he freaked out and refused to go down."

"Yeah, *that* sounds more like the Brian I met. All talk and no action." Mel patted my thigh. "So glad this wasn't Brian, but how did you end up rappelling down with a bartender? One with a fabulous physique, no less. And, uh, how did you two end up in a lip-lock? A bartender doesn't seem like your type either."

Hearing her say Paul wasn't my type caused a knot to form in my belly and my forehead wrinkled. "Why isn't he my type?"

Mel held her palms up. "Don't get in a tizzy. You seem like you'd go for someone more like—"

"Paul DeWitt?" I said, cringing at the sound of my ex's name.

"Well, yeah." Mel shrugged. "White-collar businessman. Country club member. Minus the whole cheating part."

I leaned back against the couch, pulled one of the decorative couch pillows onto my lap, and threw my hand in the air. "Who knows what my type is? I didn't even want to date in the first place."

"Are you and the bartender dating?"

"His name is Paul and no." Although, maybe I could ask him on a date. We had kissed, after all. And the kiss had been amazing.

Mel rubbed her hand against her temple. "Let me get this straight. You don't want to date, but you're going on five dates so Kristen and Ginger will help you paint. And you're not interested in any of the guys you're dating, but you kissed the only guy you're *not* dating and his name is Paul. Is that right?"

"Yes," I said, having a hard time believing the chaos resulting from two dates. All I'd wanted was to make my new home a relaxing oasis.

"Please tell me the bartender's last name isn't

DeWitt."

I racked my brain. "I have no idea what his last name is. I don't even know him."

Yet, I couldn't stop thinking about him.

Mel spread her fingers across her cell phone screen then held it up to show me the zoomed-in photo of Paul kissing me. "Looks like you know part of him up close and personal. Woo-baby, that is hot!"

Mel was right. The photo was hot. His hands gripping my waist. My hand speared through that thick tousled hair pulling him closer. And our mouths devouring each other. . . .

Staring at our personal moment plastered on the Internet made me feel exposed. Like that camera had exposed me to all of Sacramento, which it had. Sigh. "My mom's going to freak when she sees this."

Mel tilted her head thoughtfully. "Not if she thinks you're smooching Brian Burnside."

"But I'm not going out with Brian again. Ever." I squeezed the pillow in my lap. "When we finished rappelling, we landed in the Geoffries' garden patio—which was free of reporters, thankfully—and Brian was waiting for me so I had to join him for our free four-star dinner."

Mel's brows quirked. "Don't look for sympathy here. I had mac and cheese tonight."

"But I wanted to have dinner with Paul," I said, finding it hard to believe I'd just admitted that aloud.

"The new Paul?"

"Exactly."

Mel nodded. "Just making sure."

"But I can't fall for a flirty bartender. I won't. That would be like begging for a broken heart." I shook my head. "No, it's much safer remodeling my house."

"Speaking of . . ." Her face lit up and she reached into her large handbag, "Tada! Happy housewarming."

Surprised, I glanced at the rectangular white box in her hands. "For me? You didn't have to get me anything."

She handed the box to me and clapped her hands together. "I couldn't resist."

My heart swelled at Mel's thoughtfulness. I broke the gold seal on the box, and pulled out the sea-foam blue vase I'd admired at the boutique shop in Old Sac. "Mel! I can't believe you went back for this."

"I had to." She popped up excited, taking the vase

with her and placing it onto the dark bookshelf across the room. "I knew it would go perfectly here. See?"

The sea-foam blue vase looked amazing on the dark wood, and it was complimented further by the black and white Swan Lake Ballet poster I had framed next to the bookshelf. The ballet my dad had taken me to on our first father-daughter visit after he'd moved out.

I glanced back and forth between the poster and the vase as I realized that if my parents hadn't divorced—a phantom ache sliced through me thinking back to that time—then I wouldn't have Melanie for a sister. My eyes welled. Oh the irony of life.

Mel's face tensed and she hurried back, then put her hand on mine. "Do you not like the vase anymore?"

"No, I love it." My mouth spread into a small smile. "And I love you."

She pulled me into a hug. "Right back at you, sis."

****

To text or not to text, that was the question.

I stared at the square paper napkin containing ten seemingly harmless digits. I'd confessed to Mel that Paul had given me his number. She'd promptly searched the area code online, determined he's from Southern

California, then insisted that I call him tonight.

Ten digits. One phone. Tough decision.

I stood and circled the coffee table, eyeing the cell and the square napkin suspiciously. Then I dropped back down on the couch and sank into the cushions.

What harm could it cause to send one friendly text? The man had rappelled down a building for me so I wouldn't have to go alone. So romantic!

Oh, please. I gripped the sides of my hair. It hadn't been for romance. The guy bartended at the hotel. He'd probably just been looking for an excuse to ditch work for an hour. Maybe he'd even received brownie points for helping a freaked out customer (*moi*).

Then again, maybe not.

I'd just text him. Yes, I would. One text. To be polite. Even my mom would approve of good manners.

Before I could change my mind, I whipped up my phone, and typed: *Thank you for rappelling down the building with me.*

After I hit send, I gritted my teeth. How lame was that text? I hadn't even signed my name. He probably won't know who sent the message and he'll ignore it. Or delete it. Or—

Ping! Ping!

I ran my finger along my screen to find a return message from the ten-digit Southern California phone number: *Anytime, Kaitlin.*

Fueled by the zing that zipped through me, I bit my bottom lip and joked back: *Anytime? How about now?*

My entire body froze. Had I really just sent that? What if he thought I was serious? That kiss had seriously scrambled my brain and—

What's the address?

Biting my lip, I tapped out: *My house is only one-story. And I don't have rope.*

There. Safe. Close call.

Ping! Ping!

Running my finger across my screen, I read: *How about I bring over that surplus tile we talked about? See if you like it? I would've shown it to you earlier, but you decided to have dinner with your friend.*

Reassuring myself his visit was only for the good of my backyard, I typed out my address and hit send.

My phone pinged: *On my way.*

I dropped the phone like it was on fire. Paul was on his way over. To my house. At night. My heart started pounding in my ears. Freaking out much? Me? Okay, maybe a LOT.

Since Mel had prodded me to call him, I quickly texted her: *You told me to text Paul and now he's coming over. Help!*

Sitting on my couch, my knees bounced as I waited for my sister's sage advice.

After what felt like eons, my cell pinged. I brushed my finger across the screen and read: *Don't panic. You'll be fine. Just change out of those awful sweats.*

My eyes shot to my outfit and the paint splattered on my tee-shirt and sweatpants. Yikes!

Thanks. I typed back, then popped up to make a dash to my closet when I heard my cell ping again.

PS Don't forget the lip-gloss. Judging from that photo, you'll need it.

Quickly, I typed back: *He's just bringing tile over to show me. It's for the remodel.*

Although I reassured myself this visit was only for the good of my house, I searched through my makeup drawer for my lip-gloss then slid it over my lips.

Just in case.

Chapter Six

The wall clock read nine o'clock when my doorbell rang for the second time. Even though it wasn't a date, just a chance to acquire tile at a discounted price, I'd tried on and discarded multiple outfits until a mountain of clothes sat where my bed should be. I shut my bedroom door to cover the chaos, then hurried to the front door wearing a sleeveless top and black capris.

I pulled open my front door, then felt an unexpected jolt through my chest when Paul's mesmerizing eyes stared back at me. "H-Hi."

"Hi." His mouth curved up and he handed me what looked like a very expensive bottle of wine. "For your nightly tradition of wine by your dock."

I bit my bottom lip, touched that he'd remembered my favorite routine. "Except I've been on hiatus due to dating week."

He winked at me. "Maybe it's time you got back on track."

"My life's perfectly on track." Not. Everything about Paul had thrown my world completely *off* track. But his coming over was purely platonic and he'd brought over a bottle of wine so how rude would it be not to offer him some? "Thank you for the wine. Should I get us some glasses?"

"Sounds good." He followed me to the kitchen, dropped a small black bag on the counter, then surveyed the kitchen and the living room since it was an open floor plan. "I like your place."

"Thanks." I loved my open floor plan and vaulted ceilings, but my eyes zeroed in on all the work that needed to be done—new light fixtures, hardwood floors that needed refinishing, and especially the exposed walls that needed texturing and paint. "It'll be even better after this weekend."

He smirked. "Right. Free labor."

"Exactly." I opened one of the cupboards, pulled out two wine glasses, then fished in a drawer for the wine opener. "Must be hard living in a hotel. Are you looking for your own place?"

His face registered a strange look. "I'm comfortable for now."

"But it can't be homey living in a hotel, even one as nice as the Geoffries." I twisted the screw into the brown cork. "And it must be expensive. I hope they're giving you an employee discount."

He opened his mouth as if to say something, but must've changed his mind because he closed it, waited several seconds, then shrugged. "It's affordable."

His tone suggested he was holding something back, but I didn't want to pry. Plus, I was having trouble getting the cork to come out so that took all my concentration. I tugged and tugged to no avail.

"Let me." Paul eased around the counter and came up behind me. But instead of taking the bottle, he reached around me and placed his hands over mine.

"I forgot you're a professional," I said, barely able to get the words out since I was trying not to hyperventilate from the warmth of his chin against the side of my cheek, and the delicious scent of his spicy aftershave that I wanted to bottle up and keep. "How long have you been bartending?"

"Not long." He wiggled the cork out of the bottle with a gentle *pop*. "What line of work are you in?"

I made the mistake of glancing up behind me where Paul's gorgeous blues were intent on mine and our mouths were mere centimeters apart. My stomach flipped and I had the strong urge to press my mouth to his. Instead, I stepped aside. "I'm the H.R. Manager at Woodward Systems Corp downtown."

He nodded, then poured the burgundy wine. "H.R. seems like the perfect fit for you."

"How so?" I said, curious as to what he thought of me.

Handing me a glass, he said, "You seem like a woman who follows the rules and likes things in order." Then the side of his mouth curved upward and an adorable dimple formed. "At least most of the time."

Definitely not right now since every part of me wanted to break all my rules, slip my arms around Paul, and pick up where we'd left off in that photo. That would so *not* be for the remodel. "May I see the tile now?"

"First show me the area by the dock where you want to use it. So I can make sure we have enough leftover tiles to cover the space." His eyes glinted mischievously, then he lifted his wine glass up. "To your remodel and making your home exactly the way you want it."

I clinked my glass to his. "Thank you."

His eyes held mine as he brought his glass to his mouth.

I watched him as I sipped, remembering how his mouth had felt against mine. A shiver ran through me. No! I would *not* let myself fall under his spell. Focus, Kaitlin. F.O.C.U.S.

My mouth curved up into a polite smile. "Shall we go?"

He smiled back, then lifted the small black bag over his shoulder. "Lead the way."

Wine in hand, I strode through my living room to the sliding door, then slipped my toes into my flip-flops. I turned on the backyard lights, then Paul fell in line beside me as we walked across my lawn then down the railroad-tie steps, lit on either side by tiny lampposts. We made our way to the base edge of my property by the river with my beloved—and badly weathered—small wooden table and two Adirondack chairs.

Bringing Paul to my happy place worried me. I'd always come alone before. What if I lost the magic by sharing it with him? But as soon as I saw the water, the peaceful feeling washed over me. I closed my eyes, savoring the serenity, then turned to find Paul studying me. "What do you think?"

"It's definitely special." He turned to check out the

area under the dim light of two large lampposts. A splay of rocks reached out toward the calm, glassy river. Bushes and trees scattered along either side of the water. "I can see why you love it here."

I smiled, then curled up in an Adirondack, and watched him. "Think there's enough tile?"

"Should be plenty." He made long strides across the perimeter as if taking measurements, then he sat next to me and pulled out a gorgeous, terra-cotta tile from his bag. "I assume you want to cover this entire rectangular area over the dead grass?"

"That's the plan." Turning toward him, I ran my fingers over the smooth, earthy surface. "It's beautiful and looks expensive. I'm not sure I'll be able to afford it."

"Don't worry." He winked. "The hotel gives me a great discount."

I set the tile on the small table between us. "Since this week is the last of my dating deal, I'm also on my own for figuring out how to lay tile."

He twisted toward me. "I know a contractor who would make you a good deal. Let me look into it."

"That's really nice of you to help me out, Paul."

Yeah, too nice. There had to be something wrong with this guy. "What's your worst flaw?"

The corner of his mouth twitched. "You trying to paint me as a bad guy?"

"Just trying to figure you out." Nice. Charming. Handsome. And an amazing kisser. No guy could be this perfect. He was probably like every other man who seemed great at first, then as soon as you dug deeper you found out he'd been dating your sister on the side. "Take your last girlfriend, for example. What was her biggest complaint about you?"

His grin deepened. "Virna? We're still friends. Do you want to call and ask her?"

"No, I don't want to call Virna." What kind of name was that, anyway? The only Virna I'd ever heard of was the one who had won an Oscar last year for her role in that blockbuster flick about the domestically abused woman. "You must have done something wrong with Virna. Why else would you two break-up?"

His face sobered. "She wanted a ring, but I couldn't marry her. She's a wonderful person, just not who I saw spending my life with."

"Oh." That sounded so . . . reasonable. I removed a

speck of lint on my pants, then lifted my lashes.

He tilted his head. "Why did you and your ex break-up?"

My spine stiffened, but it was a fair question since I'd asked the same about him.

I took a deep breath. "Paul cheated on me. With my sister. But she didn't know he and I were together. I found out about them at my bachelorette party." To maintain my composure, I forced a small chuckle, then lifted my glass. "Not exactly the fairytale ending I'd imagined."

"I'm sorry." He watched me sip my drink, but didn't laugh at my joke. "How long has it been?"

I swallowed, staring at the sliver of wine left in my glass. "Four and a half months."

His gaze held mine and his voice softened. "I can see how that would make you adverse to dating again."

My throat tightened and the understanding apparent in his deep, blue eyes caused the block around my heart to wiggle. Not good. "Yeah, well. Three more dates and I'm done."

My voice sounded resolute, but my mind whispered that Paul could be different.

No way. He *had* to be hiding something. Hmm. . . Mother-in-laws were notoriously scary. "Was your mom disappointed you didn't marry Virna?"

He ran his fingers over a loose strand of hair that had fallen along my cheek, then tapped my nose playfully. "My mom understood and they still keep in touch."

"Really?" His mom must be seriously sweet to keep in contact with his ex. Huh.

"You sound surprised." He set his empty glass down then leaned across the table, his knuckles brushing my elbow. "Like you were hoping to find dark skeletons."

Tingles prickled up my arm. "Hoping is a strong word."

Yet, an accurate one.

He smiled, then his face grew serious. "When I commit myself to a woman for the rest of my life, it's going to be for the right reasons. I'll spend every day proving to her I know how lucky I am to have her."

A zing zipped through me.

He tucked the loose strand behind my ear. "My parents were in love their entire marriage. I won't settle for anything less."

I could see passion in his eyes when he spoke. I could

feel the solid heat, too. But he'd said "were." "Your parents aren't together anymore?"

Divorced like mine. And half the other marriages out there. Figured.

"My dad died three months ago." Emotion filled his voice and he stood, holding out his hand. "I moved up here to be close to my mom. To take care of her."

"I'm so sorry." My throat tightened and I slipped my hand into his. My mind raced as we walked slowly toward the water. "Was there . . . an accident?"

"Heart failure as a result of his diabetes." He stopped at the water's edge, laced his fingers through mine, then turned to me. "It meant a lot to me to rappel down that building with you. In more ways than one."

I squeezed my hand against his. "It meant a lot to me, too."

Standing close together, we gazed into each other's eyes, and my heart ached for his loss. He'd so clearly loved his dad. Guilt flooded through me over keeping my dad at a distance since he and my mom divorced. Even if he lived out of state, I was lucky to still have him and should appreciate that each and every day.

Paul rocked our hands gently back and forth. "So you

like the tile?"

I nodded. "Love it. Thanks for bringing it over."

He stared at me, brushing my cheek with his other hand. "You're welcome."

Those gorgeous eyes were making my stomach do floppy things again. No, I couldn't fall for him. But I so wanted to. . . .

My heart rate kicked up and I sucked in a breath. "We should probably head up."

"Good idea." The corner of his mouth turned up and he released my hand, then tapped my nose again.

I let out the breath I'd been holding. Close call. Way too close. As Paul put the tile back in his bag, I gathered our glasses and realized something. I turned toward him accusingly, and gestured with the glass I held. "At the Geoffries, you told me you'd rappelled down a building before."

Slinging his bag over his shoulder, he smirked. "You asked me if I'd rappelled before and I said you were in good hands. And you were."

We started walking and I bumped my shoulder into his teasingly. "That's totally playing with words."

"Yet still the truth." He laughed as he opened the

sliding door so I could pass through. "You made it down safely, didn't you?"

"Barely," I said, immediately thinking of our kiss. The kiss that had been uploaded to the Internet. I wondered if he'd seen the article.

He closed the door behind us. "Next time I'll make sure it's more than barely."

I smiled over my shoulder then set the glasses on the kitchen counter. "Next time I'll make sure not to date a man with a weak stomach."

"Who is lucky date number three?" He toyed with the cork on the counter as he waited for my answer.

"Kyle Harper?" Hearing myself say it as a question made me laugh. "My friend Ellen set me up."

His brows came together. "What do you know about him?"

I walked Paul to the door, then turned the handle. "I know he's getting me one day closer to free labor, which is all I need to know."

A look of relief crossed his face and he stepped through the doorway and onto the porch mat before turning back. "How is your friend Kristen doing? She going to be able to help you this weekend?"

I leaned against the doorjamb. "I'm not sure. I didn't return messages this evening. My sister, Melanie, came over before you and brought me that vase as a housewarming gift."

His eyes flicked over my shoulder toward the gorgeous sea-foam blue vase. "You've had a busy night. I should let you get some rest."

"Thanks again for bringing over the tile." I smiled appreciatively then tapped the black bag he was holding. "Let me know when you hear back about the cost."

"I will." His gaze held mine as he stepped forward, cupped my face with both hands, then brushed his thumbs over my cheeks. "You have a nice date tomorrow night."

My heart pounded and a rush of butterflies stormed my belly. "Okay," I whispered.

Then he leaned forward slowly and pressed his mouth to mine. My heart fluttered as he brushed feathery-soft kisses across my lips, so warm and gentle a small sound escaped me and I felt light-headed.

With one final sweet kiss he pulled away. "Good night."

"Good night." I bit my bottom lip as he walked toward the curb, then I closed the door and leaned back against the hard surface.

I'd tried to prove that Paul wasn't perfect and had failed miserably.

My heart was so in trouble.

Chapter Seven

I arrived at work Wednesday morning and found Ellen Holbrook waiting in my office—more like sleeping, actually. She wore a peach button-up maternity dress that showed off her adorable baby bump. Her eyes were closed and her hand rested protectively over her ballooning belly.

Seeing her wedding ring sparkle on her finger caused that image of Paul wearing a tuxedo to pop into my head. His gorgeous blues and his flirty personality had been all I could think about until last night. Now all I could think about was his feathery-soft kisses that made me melt.

And made my nerves go on red alert.

Clearing my throat loudly, I sat at my desk. "Good morning, Ellen."

Her eyes popped open, and she brought a hand to her cheek. "Kaitlin? Sorry, I must've dozed off."

I chuckled. "Baby kicking all night again?"

Her mouth stretched into a smile. "Yes, he's going to be quite the soccer player."

"You found out the sex?" I'd thought they'd decided

to wait.

"No, I just meant he as in the baby, in general. Henry thinks it'll be fun to be surprised and I don't want to ruin that for him." Her mouth went tight. "Not like he's the one who's going to have a baby shower with only gender-neutral colors, though."

"I, uh . . ." I blinked, stunned. I'd never heard Ellen utter a single negative word about her hubby. He sounded so perfect I thought he was fictional. Her lack of sleep must be getting to her. That or hormones. "What can I help you with?"

"The FMLA paperwork for my maternity leave." She pushed a small stack of papers toward me. "And Kristen."

My eyes shot up from the paperwork. Kristen had left me a voicemail last night ranting that if Ellen didn't get off her back about her mother she might lose it. "Don't tell me the engagement is off. I know she's been stressing—"

"It's still on for eighteen months from now. That's the problem." She straightened, tried crossing her legs over her bubble belly several times, then finally gave up. "We have to convince Kristen not to listen to her mother."

Since their close friendship went way back to high school, I knew Ellen meant well. But Kristen's voicemail made it clear she wanted Ellen to lay off. "I don't think that's wise."

Ellen stared at me like I'd grown a third head. "Kristen's mom cares more about *where* they get married than her daughter marrying the man she loves. It's all about appearances, not marriage."

"Her mom may be difficult," I said, thinking of my own mother, "but she loves Kristen and only wants her wedding to be as beautiful as possible. Eighteen months isn't that long."

Ellen huffed. "It could be a lifetime. We have no guarantees in life."

Even Paul's parents' time together had been cut short, but that wasn't the point. "She doesn't want to hurt her mom. I think we should respect her decision."

She scoffed. "If I'd listened to my own mom, I'd still be online dating instead of with the love of my life."

Yikes. That would've been a tragedy since they were the perfect couple (minus the baby-gender decision). "Kristen's mom isn't against Ethan. She just wants the best wedding for them."

Ellen shook her head. "She wants the best *appearance* and, yes, the Geoffries ballroom is amazing. I'd looked into renting the room as well, but declined due to the wait list. There are plenty of other perfectly acceptable wedding locations that are booking only two months out. I know because that's what I did last year."

A valid point. "Even if I agreed with you, Kristen would never break her mother's heart like that."

She banged her index finger against the desk. "This wedding shouldn't be about what her mother wants. It's about Kristen and Ethan committing themselves to each other and becoming family. She needs to stand up to her mother once and for all."

The thought of standing up to my own mother terrorized me. "It'll never happen. Kristen's practical like me. She may not be marrying Ethan in the time frame she wants, but they'll be married in eighteen months and then everyone will be happy."

Her brows came together and her eyes went wild and crazy. "Until her mother decides Kristen shouldn't know the sex of her own baby and then what's she supposed to do? Give in again? When does it end? When does she get to live the life *she* wants?"

My mouth dropped open. "Um. . ."

"Right. Um." Ellen leaned back in her chair, looking like she needed another nap after that passionate speech. "We have to talk to her. Convince her that getting married when she wants and where she wants is the right thing to do."

I shook my head. "It'll never happen, sweetie."

Holding onto the table for support, she pushed to her feet. "Well, I'm going to try."

I nodded, watching her waddle her way to the door. "Hey, Ellen?"

"Yeah?"

I bit my bottom lip. "You should tell Henry how badly you want to know the sex of the baby. It's shouldn't be only about what the daddy wants but what the mommy wants as well."

She blinked as I pointed out her own logic. "You're right. I'm going to talk to him. Thanks, Kaitlin. And have fun on your date with Kyle tonight. He's a keeper."

"Sure. See you later." My phone rang and I snatched up the receiver. "Kaitlin Murray."

"Are you free for lunch today?" Kristen's voice

shrilled across the line. "I need to talk to you. It's about the wedding."

Oh, no. What now? I glanced at my calendar. "I can meet you at noon. Where?"

Kristen let out a breath. "Wok N' Roll in Old Sac."

"I'll be there." I hung up the phone and had the strange feeling something huge had happened. I just hoped the wedding was still on.

****

As soon as the waiter at Wok N' Roll left with our lunch orders, Kristen turned to me with what I can only describe as a maniacal grin. "This is where Ethan and I are getting married. I'm so excited."

I surveyed the casual Chinese restaurant then pulled my chin back, thoroughly confused. "You mean in Old Sac?"

Kristen shook her head. "Here, at Wok N' Roll."

My mouth dropped open. She seemed serious. I had no words.

She held her hands up. "After Ellen left last night, I walked around my condo—the one I decorated to perfection when I gave it my obsessive home make-over after Jake and I broke-up—and reality hit me. Even though I love my place, I don't want to live there for the next eighteen months alone."

I reached for my water, guzzled, then set the glass back down and pointed out the obvious. "You're not alone. You have Gina."

She cackled as if I'd said the funniest thing. "Gina's a fabulous roommate. I meant I don't want to live without Ethan."

What happened to not wanting to hurt her mother?

My head spun from Kristen's one-eighty, the fact that she was planning her dream wedding at a Chinese restaurant, and that her normally calm demeanor had been replaced by a personality resembling a Kewpie doll gone mad. "Um, is there a historical significance to this place that I'm not aware of?"

Her grin appeared frozen as she shook her head. "No, but there is a party room in back and availability in six weeks, which is when I'm going to marry Ethan."

Okay, I was just going to say it. Someone had to be the voice of reason. "You can't have your wedding here."

Kristen blinked as if surprised. "Why not?"

Did she want me to make a list? Okay, I could do that.

I held one finger out at a time. "One, because it smells like chow mein in here. Two, soy sauce will not come out of a wedding dress. And three, a fortune cookie is *not* a wedding cake."

She snapped her fingers. "I hadn't thought of fortune cookies. We'll put our names and the date on those slips of paper inside the cookies."

That actually sounded cute. . . .

I shook my head to clear the thought. "Do you really want to walk down the aisle past a fish tank with a neon sign above it reading 'Nobody woks it like we do'?"

She tilted her head. "They have availability in six weeks. I'm getting married here and there's nothing you or my mother can say to talk me out of it."

"If I thought you really wanted to get married here, I'd support you. I just think you're being rash and—" My mouth froze as Kristen's handsome fiancé entered the restaurant with another woman. A gorgeous woman. She wore a designer pants suit, her hair was pulled back into a low and tight ponytail, and her sharp, no-nonsense expression warned everyone not to mess with her.

And she was with Ethan! My heart sank and I wanted to cry.

Kristen gave me an odd look then turned over her shoulder to where I was staring. Instead of gritting her teeth or freaking out, she lifted her hand and waved.

Ethan smiled back. Not exactly the look of someone getting caught cheating.

Perhaps I'd jumped to conclusions. . . .

Ethan said something to the woman, then they came over to our table. He leaned down and kissed Kristen on the cheek. "Hi, honey. Kaitlin."

I gave a little wave.

"I'd like you both to meet Jill Parnell. She works with Charlie over at Corbett, Grey, and Shaw. We're meeting him for lunch and thought it would be fun to run into you here."

Kristen smiled, and held her hand out to Jill. "Nice to meet you."

Instead of biting her head off like the shark she appeared to be, Jill accepted Kristen's hand with a warm smile. "You, too."

Again, I waved.

"Have a good lunch." Kristen smiled then turned back to me as Ethan and Jill strode toward the entrance to meet up with the man who'd just walked in. "Charlie's a good friend of Ethan's. They're talking about opening their own law firm together."

"Sounds like an exciting move." Glancing around me, I bit my lip. "Back to the wedding location, though. I'm afraid you're making a mistake Kristen. I know you won't be happy disappointing your mom like this."

"You and I have a lot in common when it comes to mothers, Kaitlin." Kristen leaned back as the waiter set our dishes down. "But I've changed since I met Ethan. Love makes you willing to take huge risks because the payoff is so worth it. I could marry him in a tent and it would still be the best day of my life. My mom is going to have to deal."

I immediately thought of Paul. He wasn't the country club type my mom had always pushed me toward, but I loved being around him. Maybe he'd be worth taking a risk for.

She slid her chopsticks into her stir fried rice. "We don't get many second chances in life and Ethan is my second chance. You have a beautiful house . . . do you really want to be in it alone forever?"

"Until this week I would've answered yes." But relaxing with Paul by the dock hadn't taken me out of my happy place—sharing the space with him had made it better. Warmer. Fuller.

"And now?"

"I'm going on date number three tonight." I glanced over to where Ethan was having lunch with the beautiful brunette. Like me, Kristen had been cheated on before. But she hadn't had one ounce of jealousy seeing Ethan with that gorgeous attorney because she trusted him. I made a decision. "I'm also going to line up date number four."

Kristen's brows quirked. "With who?"

My heart rate picked up just thinking about him. "The bartender from the Geoffries hotel."

There, I'd said it. There was no turning back.

Tonight, I'd ask Paul on a date. I just hoped he said yes.

****

After work, I strode into the Geoffries hotel to meet date number three. Yes, I'd picked the location but Kyle had *asked* where I wanted to go and the hotel seemed convenient since I needed to seal date number four as soon as possible (before I freaked out and changed my mind). It felt too impersonal to ask Paul out via telephone, which was why I'd arrived at the hotel early for my date.

Checking my watch, my heels clicked across the lobby as I headed for the bar.

"Kaitlin?"

I stopped in the middle of the marble lobby, tingles running down my spine at the familiar male voice. I glanced over my shoulder and, sure enough, Paul stood behind the concierge desk wearing his sexy grin.

I couldn't stop the smile that spread over my face or the happiness that filled me at the sight of him. I walked over to the desk, then placed my purse on the counter. "What are you doing here?"

His eyes crinkled. "Working."

"That's obvious." I laughed. "But what are you doing here at the concierge desk and not over there at the bar?"

He leaned over the desk. "Filling in. Manuel has the night off."

Shooting him a questioning look, I teased, "Isn't being a concierge a form of art? Like in that Michael J. Fox movie, *For Love or Money?*"

He smirked. "You don't think I can handle it?"

"I'm not sure." I leaned toward him and breathed in

his spicy scent. "You do make a mean Geoffries Martini though."

"If you take a break from your date, I'll have one here waiting for you," he said, then straightened and stepped back.

I frowned. "But—"

"Kaitlin Murray?" a male voice said from behind me.

I swiveled around. "Yes?"

In front of me stood a tall, muscular, blond who could easily rival any Greek god. I take that back. With that crown of gold, athletic build, and sparkling green eyes, he might actually *be* a Greek god—if one had descended to Sacramento wearing a polo shirt, that is.

"Kyle Harper." He thrust his hand out. "I recognized you from the photo Ellen showed me."

Wow, Ellen hadn't told me Kyle Harper was hot.

"You're early." My forehead wrinkled at my date's promptness. I hadn't asked Paul out yet and what if he got off work before I had the chance? How late did a temp concierge work, anyway?

When I continued to stand there, Kyle gave me an odd look. "Shall we go?"

Since it seemed rude to ask him to hold on a sec

while I checked to see if the concierge was free tomorrow night, I smiled politely. "Sure."

As we sauntered off, I glanced back at Paul and shot him an apologetic look. He did not, however, pass me a look of understanding. In fact, his jaw muscles tightened, and the usual glint in his eyes disappeared.

****

Kyle had made a reservation so we were seated right away in a corner table next to an indoor waterfall. When the waitress took our drink order, I asked for water only. I figured no drinks, no appetizer, and no dessert might speed this date up.

Unfortunately, Kyle didn't seem worried about time because he ordered a beer. Sigh.

"How long have you known Ellen?" Kyle asked.

"A few months." I glanced behind me in the direction of the lobby as if I might be able to see Paul through some kind of x-ray vision. Didn't work.

Kyle opened his menu, but kept his eyes on me. "She said you two work together?"

"Mmhmm." I opened my own menu, chose the first thing I spotted, then shut it again. "You ready to order?"

"Not quite yet," he said, slowly. He gave me a

curious look then began perusing the menu.

After a few seconds, my knees started bouncing. Why was it taking Kyle forever to pick a dish? It's not like the menu was *that* big. I eyed him closely, wondering if he'd notice if I sent a quick text under the table.

He glanced up from his menu and caught me staring. Oh, yeah. He'd notice.

"Everything all right, Kaitlin?"

"Great." I drummed my fingers against the table. "The shrimp scampi looks good."

"I'll keep that in mind." His brows rose as he turned back to the menu.

The waitress arrived with our drinks. "Are you ready to order?"

Kyle opened his mouth—

"Yes, I'll have the shrimp scampi please." My head whipped to my date. "Kyle?"

He set his menu down and leaned back. "May I hear your specials?"

My neck stiffened. Did this guy have all the time in the world or what?

"Excuse me a minute while I run to the . . . restroom." I slid out of the booth and raced down the stairs before either could answer me. As I hurried toward the lobby, I straightened my silk top then ran my fingers down my hair as I tried to work up the courage to ask Paul on a date—if he hadn't gotten off work, that is.

I flew past the bar, down the corridor, and let out a sigh of relief when I spotted him behind the concierge desk. Another employee stood next to him and I recognized the woman from rappelling last night. Odd that she'd worked with him on the fifth floor and now happened to be working at the concierge desk with him today. She didn't so much as glance at me as I trotted up, but then again she was helping a guest.

"You're back," he said, when I stopped in front of him.

"Sorry. My date arrived early." I rolled my eyes in a way that said 'whatever.' "So we didn't get to finish our conversation."

And I didn't get to ask him out on a date yet. Gulp.

His face relaxed and his mouth curved upward as he whipped out a martini glass and shaker from below his desk and poured me a pink drink that had to be a Geoffries Martini. "As promised."

Just what I needed to give my courage a little boost.

"You are the most thoughtful concierge slash bartender ever."

He brushed his lips over my ear. "Sweetheart, you haven't seen anything yet."

A shiver ran through me. Oh *wow*.

I brought the martini glass to my lips, sipped my drink, and the cold, sweet liquid rolled down my throat. "Delicious. What's in it?"

He shook his head. "Can't tell you. It's a Geoffries family secret."

I guffawed. "It's not like the Geoffries are real people."

He chuckled. "You think they're alien imposters?"

"No." I giggled. "I guess I never thought about it. I just drink at the hotel—"

"And rappel . . ."

"Exactly." I touched his forearm and his ropey muscles flexed under my fingers.

He glanced at my hand as I (regretfully) removed it from his arm. "I can tell you that this martini was named after Irene Geoffries. It's her favorite drink, and her husband would bring her a glass every night while she cooked them dinner."

"Sounds romantic." I took another sweet sip. "My husband would never do that for me because I rarely cook."

Had I just said husband? When had I put the idea of marriage back on the table?

Paul reached out to play with a lock of my hair. "I'd bring you a drink every night. You could probably convince me to cook for you, too."

Staring into his ethereal eyes, my stomach flipped. I knew this was my chance. I mean, he must like me if he was twirling my hair between his manly fingers and offering (hypothetically) to bring me drinks à la romantic hotel magnate, Mr. Geoffries.

I swallowed, then blurted. "Would you be my date number four tomorrow night?"

Momentary surprise flickered across his face, then he shook his head. "No, I don't think that's a good idea."

My heart sank. "Why not?"

His eyes twinkled. "Aren't you *on* a date right now?"

"Oh, Kyle!" I drained half my martini, then set it back down. "I'd better get back because he was ordering dinner and—"

"Wait." He reached into the inside pocket of his suit

jacket and pulled out two tickets. "Want to go with me to the ballet tonight?"

My head spun. "Are you asking me out on a date?"

He shook his head. "No, it's just for fun. One of the perks of being concierge is that I have two extra tickets to see Cinderella."

I tilted my head. "You like the ballet?"

His eyes held amusement. "Who *doesn't* like the ballet?"

Me, for one. The only time I'd gone was when my dad had taken me after my parents split and I'd spent the entire time trying not to cry. But that had been over a decade ago. And being next to Paul in a dark theatre didn't exactly sound horrible. Maybe I could even let him know what he was missing by rejecting me. . . .

I took a final sip of my Geoffries Martini (yum). "I'm in."

His face lit up. "Great. Meet here in an hour?"

"All right." I hurried across the lobby, past the bar, and up the stairs to the restaurant. I found Kyle leaning back in his seat with half his beer gone. "Sorry. That took longer than expected."

I cringed. That did not sound pretty.

Kyle sipped his beer, then set it back down. "You're obviously not interested in me, Kaitlin. That's really okay—"

"No, you're great." I shook my head quickly. "In fact, I'd love to set you up on a date with my friend Ginger."

His forehead wrinkled. "Aren't *we* on a date?"

Oh, this was awkward.

"Yes. . ." My voice trailed off and I cringed, realizing it was time to come clean. "I'm sorry, but I only agreed to go out with you because of my friends. I told them I wasn't ready to date and they pushed me to get back in the game so I made a dating deal, which wasn't fair to you. Then I met this guy who works for the hotel and I didn't mean to, but I think I've fallen for him. You're super nice and incredibly handsome and I didn't mean to waste your time."

Instead of getting annoyed or angry, he laughed. "Handsome and nice? That has got to be the best rejection speech ever."

Feeling like a louse, I raised my brow. "You're not upset?"

"Actually, I am." He flashed a smile, showing off his straight white teeth. "If you're interested in this other guy, what are you doing here with me? Go get him, Kaitlin."

Who was I to argue with a Greek god?

Chapter Eight

I stared at my reflection in the silver-framed mirror of the Geoffries hotel's women's lounge and touched up my lip-gloss. Remembering Paul's kiss last night, I shivered. Why wouldn't he go out with me? No guy could kiss like that if he wasn't into someone. No way. At least I didn't think so. . . .

My *wind chimes* ring tone sounded so I pulled my cell out and glanced at the number. Mom. Since it was her second call today, I had to answer or she'd worry.

"Hi, Mom. How are you?"

"I've been frantic all day, thank you very much." There was a long pause. "Did you not receive my voicemail this morning?"

The one she'd left about my date with Brian Burnside? "Yes, I got it."

Another pause. Mom loved to make people wait so she'd be sure to have our full attention. "Then why in the world haven't you phoned me back?"

"I've been busy." That and I was afraid she'd seen the Internet photo and determined that kiss had *not* been with Brian. Gulp. "Everything all right?"

"Yes, now that I know my daughter is still alive." She waited a few beats. "I'm calling because I spoke with Alisha Burnside this morning. She told me Brian raved about his date with you last night and he very much wants to take you out again. Isn't that wonderful?"

Not unless there was a new definition of the word. "I don't think Brian's my type, Mom."

"He's handsome, kind, and comes from a good family. That's exactly your type, dear."

Thinking of Kristen and how she'd stood up to her mom, I took a deep breath. "I'm actually interested in someone else." Someone who'd rejected me and could very well be seeing a horde of other women, but still. "He's sweet, charming, and has a great sense of humor."

Pause. "What's he do for a living?"

Ah, the bottom line. "He's a bartender at the Geoffries hotel."

She gasped. "I think I've just had my first coronary attack."

I cringed. "Anyway, I have to go because he's taking me to the ballet tonight. We're seeing Cinderella."

"Darling, think of your future." Mom took a deep

breath. "Brian is stable, steady, and the better choice."

Not if I wanted someone to rappel down a building with me. Or make me smile. . . "Brian is nice and I'm sure he'll make some woman very happy."

Someone woman who was *not* me.

Short pause. "I told Alisha you would have dinner with Brian at the country club tomorrow night."

My mouth dropped open. "Why would you do that?"

She huffed. "I thought you'd thank me."

"I'm twenty-eight years old, Mom!" I shrugged apologetically at a woman coming into the powder room to wash her hands, then I lowered my voice. "I do not need you making dates for me."

The silence at the other end of the line was deafening. "Maybe you didn't hit it off right away with Brian, but what harm is there in giving him one more chance? For me?"

I glanced up as the woman glided past me with a sympathetic smile. I sighed, then remembered my remodel. I did still need a date number four and Paul *had* turned me down. "All right. But no more fixing me up."

"Wonderful, dear. You won't regret it."

Unfortunately, I already did.

****

When I arrived to the lobby, I found Paul chatting with his beautiful co-worker. He had a pen poised over a piece of paper, then he underlined something. As I approached, she glanced up at me with an odd look. Oh, great. Maybe she'd heard me ask him out earlier and also heard him reject me. If she was jonesing for him—as any sane woman would—she must be doing inner cartwheels right now.

Although she wasn't going to the ballet with him. Ha!

Feeling like I was interrupting something, I smiled awkwardly. "Hi."

Paul's head shot up. "Kaitlin? You're early."

"If you need more time I can—"

"No, it's fine." He folded the piece of paper. "Have you met Alice?"

I shook my head. "Hi, Alice."

She smiled. "Nice to meet you, Kaitlin."

Paul handed Alice the paper. "You'll take care of this for me?"

"Right away." She nodded. "Enjoy the ballet."

"We will." He came around the desk, slipped his hand into mine, and winked at me. "How was your date?"

My stomach flipped at the feel of his skin against mine. "Kyle's handsome and nice. The perfect date."

For someone else.

Paul's forehead wrinkled as the lobby doors slid open and we turned right down the sidewalk. "Are you going out with him for date number four?"

"No." I watched the crinkle on his forehead disappear. "I've already filled date number four with someone else."

His hand tightened around mine and a line formed between his brows. "With who?"

I bit my bottom lip, thoroughly confused. He was acting quite jealous for a guy who'd rejected me. "Brian Burnside."

He chuckled, his eyes lighting up. "Make sure you don't take him above the first floor."

It was my turn for furrowed brows. "At least he's willing to date me."

"And get you one step closer to free labor this weekend." He stopped at the crosswalk. "Your friends still going to help you?"

A car horn blared at a taxi as our pedestrian light illuminated. "Ginger's in for sure. I'm worried about

Kristen, though. Remember how I told you she's getting married at the Geoffries in eighteen months?"

He nodded. "Her mom insisted on the location, right? Wise choice, I might add."

"They do have an amazing staff." Even if a certain bartender refused to officially date me. "But she's decided to get married at Wok N' Roll instead."

He strode into the Sacramento Community Theatre then let go of my hand and reached into his pocket for our tickets. "The Chinese restaurant? Why?"

"They have availability in six weeks and that's when she wants to marry Ethan." I watched him hand two tickets to the usher, who gave him a program in exchange. "It makes me sad because I think she'll regret it. She's like me and wants the fairytale ending with the elegant white gown, music, to be surrounded by friends, and plumeria flowers," I added, wistfully.

He put his hand on the small of my back as we walked down the theatre aisle and the usher showed us to our seats. "Plumeria flowers?"

My face heated. Had I said that aloud? "Well, maybe not for Kristen."

"But for you?" He nodded to the usher who had

stopped in front of our row.

I smiled at the usher, slipped into my seat, then promptly opened the program.

Paul took his seat, turned toward me, then flipped the program closed. "Why plumeria flowers?"

Looking into his deep, blue eyes compelled me to open up and tell him what I'd never told anyone before. "When I was twelve, my parents took me on vacation to Kauai. Have you ever been?"

He shook his head.

"It's the most beautiful place I've ever seen. We had a condo on the ocean and I'd fall asleep listening to the waves crash against the shore. We snorkeled on the north shore of the island, boated along the Na Pali coast, strolled along the beaches, and inhaled the fragrant scent of plumeria flowers. It was the best week of my life . . . and the last time I felt safe and secure." I closed my eyes and could almost feel transported there with the fragrant scent wafting up my nose. When I opened my eyes the lights in the theatre flashed on and off. "When we got home, my parents announced they were getting a divorce, and it felt like they'd yanked the rug out from under me. My dad moved out that weekend."

His eyes stayed on mine as he brushed his knuckles along my cheekbone. "I'm sorry, sweetheart. That must've been hard."

My vision blurred as his arm slipped around me, and I lay my head against his shoulder. A warm wave of comfort washed over me, making it feel like I'd been transported back to the beach where everything was easy and life made sense. I felt . . . happy.

The lights went down and the red curtain slid open. Cinderella was starting.

****

"Kaitlin?" Paul's voice whispered against my ear and his fingers traced my cheekbone.

My skin hummed along the pathway he'd touched and I burrowed my nose into his neck. "Mmm."

He shook my shoulder gently. "Sweetheart, it's intermission."

My eyes burst open. "What?"

We were at the theatre, the lights were blaring, and a couple stood to my right looking irritated as they eyed my legs which were blocking them from getting out of our row. I popped up immediately and smoothed down my hair.

Oh, embarrassment. Nothing against the ballet but with all that graceful dancing and serene music, how did they expect me to stay awake?

Paul reached for my hand as we strode out to the lobby. "Dare I ask if you enjoyed the first act?"

"Sorry, I'm just tired." His fault, really, since I'd stayed awake too late thinking about him. "Maybe a cup of coffee would help."

He squeezed my hand then turned toward the long line at the refreshment bar. "Your wish is my command."

"Hmm. I like that." He'd taken me to the ballet, he was holding my hand, and now he was getting me an espresso drink. This sure *felt* like a date. "Are you sure this isn't a date?"

The corner of his mouth turned up. "Why are you trying to label our time together? Can't we just have fun?"

I *always* had fun when I was with him, and he seemed to enjoy being with me if the kissing and hand holding was any indication. So why wouldn't he date me? "Are you one of those guys who fears commitment?"

His smile grew. "Not at all. I prefer it."

Hmm. . . "Are you seeing someone right now?"

"No."

We stepped forward in line. "Are you still hung up on that Virna girl?"

He chuckled now. "No. She and I are over each other."

I let out an exasperated breath. "Then why—"

"Kaitlin," a woman's voice came from behind us. A refined voice that sounded eerily like my mother.

Eyes wide, I spun on my heel, and faced an older version of me. "Mom? What are you *doing* here?"

She clasped her jeweled fingers together in front of her. "I read a fabulous review on this ballet in the paper and tickets were still available online so daddy and I thought it would be fun." She smiled innocently as she turned her attention to Paul. "Aren't you going to introduce me to your friend?"

Innocently coming to the same ballet as us? Yeah, right.

My eyes narrowed. "I can't believe you—"

"I'm Paul." He let go of my hand, stepped out of line, then gathered my mom's hand in his own. "It's a pleasure to meet you . . . ?"

"Janet." Mom's smile was in place but her eyes

turned icy. "Kaitlin's mother."

"I'm Gary Porter." My stepdad shook Paul's hand, seeming oblivious of the ambush his wife had clearly planned.

Mom kept her attention on Paul. "Kaitlin tells me you're a bartender."

My jaw tightened at the way she'd said *bartender*. Like she didn't approve of his career choice. "Mother—"

"Yes, I'm a bartender. Among other things." Paul's eyes twinkled and he seemed unfazed by my mother's probing.

She raised her chin a notch. "You look familiar . . . what do your parents do? If you don't mind my asking?"

I saw Paul's gaze flicker and my chest ached knowing he was thinking of his dad. "Mom, I don't—"

"My parents have always been in the service industry." His voice was steady but the color of his eyes deepened. "But my father passed away several months ago."

"I'm sorry to hear it." Mom's icy tone softened.

I was relieved she actually seemed to mean that, so I cleared my throat. "Well, enjoy the show and we'll talk later."

And I meant that. How dare she interrogate Paul?

"And you enjoy your date tomorrow night at the country club with Brian." Mom's smile remained plastered on her face as she turned from me to Paul. "I've always wanted a fine life for my daughter, Paul. Don't you agree she deserves that?"

My face heated and I was so ready to tell my mom off—

"I completely agree with you, Janet." He held her gaze as he said the words. "Kaitlin deserves the very best life has to offer. The finest of everything."

My brows came together, partly from how they were talking about me like I wasn't here, but mostly because I didn't need *things*. I needed to be happy, content, and secure. To be able to be myself and not pretend everything's perfect all the time—the way I was with Paul.

"We're in agreement then." Mom gave Paul an icy smile as the overhead lights flickered. She laced her arm through my stepdad's. "We'd better get to our seats, dear."

"Enjoy the show." Dad nodded at Paul and me, appearing unaware of his wife's attack on Paul as they walked away.

Paul brushed his fingers over my arm. "Looks like we missed your coffee."

My eyes burned, and I didn't want to chance running into my mom a second time. "I'm sorry, but I have to go."

"We'll leave then." He put a hand on my back and made a motion toward the door.

"No." I shook my head. "You stay and enjoy the rest of the show. I don't want to ruin your entire night when you were excited to see the ballet."

The corners of his mouth turned upward. "Sweetheart, the ballet bores me out of my mind."

My jaw dropped open. "You said you loved it."

"No, I asked 'who doesn't love the ballet'?" He slipped his hand in mine and tugged me toward the exit. "And well, I would be one of those people."

"Then why would you . . . ?"

"To spend time with you." He rubbed his thumb over the back of my hand. "I saw the Swan Lake poster framed in your living room and figured you loved the ballet. I had no idea you'd fall asleep on me."

My insides glowed as I realized he hadn't had an

extra ticket to the ballet. He'd planned to take me, which must mean he was into me. Warm fuzzies fluttered in my belly.

"Thank you." I smiled up at him as we strode down the sidewalk to the hotel and where I'd parked. "I hung the poster up because my dad means a lot to me, not the ballet. He took me to Swan Lake right after my parents separated. It had been a week since he'd moved out and I'd missed him terribly. I spent the entire ballet dreading him leaving me again. Soon after, he took a job in Seattle and was gone."

He squeezed my waist as we walked. "I'm sure you were in his heart."

I sniffed. "I never thought of that before, but you're probably right. He was in mine."

We arrived to the front of the hotel and I gestured down the street. "I parked two blocks that way."

"I'll walk you."

We ambled in silence, side by side, and I thought about the night's events. I didn't know why Paul turned me down for a date if he wasn't seeing anyone else, but he *had* to have feelings for me. Just like I had feelings for him. Otherwise he wouldn't be so thoughtful and caring and sweet and have put up with my mother. . . .

Ugh. My mother.

I took a deep breath. "I'm sorry for how my mom acted earlier. I'd like to say she was having an off night, but that's actually just the way she is. She thinks she knows what's best for me, but she doesn't."

He smiled down at me. "No need to apologize. I agree with your mom."

My heart stopped as I realized she'd gotten to him. "But she's *wrong*. She thinks I need to be with an executive who has a country club membership and flies first class."

"A private jet is actually more convenient." He sounded completely serious as he said this. "You deserve that."

I stared up at him wondering what in the world he was talking about. Who cared about those kinds of things?

I gestured to my sporty coupe parked at the curb. "I'd rather have a Geoffries Martini brought to me every night. That means more than what money can buy."

"You deserve both." He walked me around to the driver's side even as I gaped at him. "I know the perfect guy to set you up with. You still need a date for Friday night, right?"

My throat tightened. "You want to set me up with someone?"

"He's perfect for you." He opened my door. "Your mom would love Milton. He meets all of her requirements."

Milton?

I stared into those gorgeous blue eyes and my heart cracked. Paul didn't have feelings for me if he could set me up with someone else, and the fact that he'd listened to my mom meant he didn't know me at all. I'd been fooling myself.

My chest ached, burned . . . as if he'd shoved a knife into it.

But I refused to let it show.

I forced a smile. "Milton sounds perfect for date number five. Thanks."

And after date number five, I was done with men.

Chapter Nine

On Thursday, my workday passed by in a blur. Ellen was shocked I didn't hit it off with Kyle, but I reminded her that I'd only entered the dating deal in exchange for Kristen and Ginger's help. Melanie had emailed the Internet photo to Ginger who'd stormed into my office and demanded details on "the building smooch." I assured Ginger the kiss meant nothing—which it hadn't to Paul, obviously.

I got another voicemail from my dad asking me to call him, but I didn't have the energy to call him back. To be honest, I barely had the energy to meet Brian for dinner at the club. It's not that he wasn't nice—although he made my head spin when he mentioned a completely new firm he supposedly worked for—it's just that I didn't have it in me to fake a smile any longer. I wanted to stick with my remodel, mellow out in my sanctuary, and keep my heart safe.

Only when I got home after my (very last) date with Brian, I dropped onto the sofa and tried to relax, but everything reminded me of Paul. The pink heels I'd kicked off as soon as I walked in the door brought back the thrill of rappelling down the Geoffries hotel with him. The half-empty wine bottle on the counter reminded me of our conversation by the river where he'd opened up to me about his dad. The ballet poster in the living room transported me back to the theatre where I'd cuddled up to him so relaxed and secure, I'd fallen asleep.

Tears burned my eyes. He'd totally intruded on my plans to remodel my house. I tried to think about paint swatches and fabric patterns and cool furniture, but all I could think about were his sapphire-blue eyes, charming smile, and teasing voice. He'd even ruined my happy place. No way I'd take a glass of wine down to the river when all I'd feel is empty that he wasn't with me.

I had my fifth date scheduled and my free labor lined up for the weekend so I should be ecstatic right now. Instead, I felt freaking miserable. If only I hadn't craved that Geoffries Martini. . . .

Wind chimes tingled and I glanced at my cell phone. Kristen.

I pressed ANSWER. "What now? Please don't tell me a certain fast food joint had wedding availability in their children's playland sooner than Wok N' Roll. I don't think I could stand you getting married in a place where shoes are optional but socks are a must."

"That's funny." Kristen laughed. "But fear not, my friend, Wok N' Roll is off."

I sat up slowly. "What do you mean by off?"

"You're not going to believe this." Kristen voice was calm and it was hard to know if I should be alarmed or not. "I just received a phone call from a woman at the Geoffries hotel. They had to relocate a charity event that had been scheduled in their ballroom for six weeks from now. Therefore, she said that date is available if Ethan and I want it. Six weeks from now, which is *exactly* when we want to get married. How incredible is that?"

My jaw dropped. "How can that be? It was booked out eighteen months from now. There has to be a long list of couples before you guys."

"Whose side are you on?" She huffed. "Do you want me to get married with chopsticks in my hair?"

"No." I laughed. "I'm just floored. That's amazing news, Kristen. I'm so happy for you. Your mom must be thrilled."

Just like my mom would be thrilled when she found out I was dating *Milton*. Blech.

"I'm going to let her stew for tonight and I'll call her tomorrow." She chuckled. "How are things with you? Your receptionist told me you went home for lunch, but I stopped by your house and there was no answer."

"I'd planned to go home for a catnap, but Mel called with good news so I met her downtown at Cherie's Café to celebrate her new job. She'll be teaching first grade at a private school starting next week."

"Good for Mel." She paused and I heard beeping in the background. "I have to go. Ethan just texted me about some family rug his mom wants us to get married on. Oh, by the way, are you getting work done on your house? There was a silver truck parked in your driveway when I came by."

"No. . ." My brows furrowed then something clicked in my mind. "Paul did say he had the name of a contractor for me. Maybe he gave him my address for a bid?"

"Paul with the dark hair and heavenly blue eyes? What ever happened with him?"

A slice of pain speared my heart. "Nothing."

"Really?" She sounded surprised. "I sensed serious chemistry between you two. And, of course, Mel showed me the photo."

I rolled my eyes toward the ceiling. "It wasn't real, okay? I'd looked five floors down and freaked, so he was just distracting me."

"Nice distraction." She made a humming noise. "Talk to you soon. Bye."

"Bye." I pressed the END button on my phone, which immediately lit up with an incoming call from my dad. Knowing I shouldn't avoid him any longer, I sighed and tapped the ANSWER button. "Hello?"

"Kaitlin, I'm glad you picked up."

I crossed my arm over my chest, feeling guilty. "I'm sorry I didn't call you back, Dad. It's been a long week. Is everything okay?"

"Yes, but there's been a slight change for tomorrow. Meetings are scheduled in the afternoon now because, well, I won't bore you with the details. Then my flight leaves at six so I'll only have time to meet you for lunch." His tone sounded apologetic. "I'll have to see the house on my next visit. Is that all right?"

Disappointment crept through me, but I was used to this when it came to my parents. "No worries, Dad. Lunch would be wonderful."

"One more thing, honey." He paused and the silence stretched out. "I'll be bringing someone with me."

Did he mean . . . ?

"Her name is Jennifer and, well," another long pause, "I'm going to ask her to marry me."

A bomb dropped in my stomach and it felt like I was twelve-years-old and he'd just announced he was moving out. I knew I should say congratulations, but. . . "I didn't even know you were dating someone."

"I didn't want to mention her until I knew for sure it would last. I'm excited for you to meet her." He waited and the silence stretched out. "I'll see you tomorrow, honey."

"Bye." I stared at my phone: *Call Ended*.

First Kristen, then Mel, and now my dad. Everyone had good news except me.

What was I doing wrong?

****

Standing outside the Geoffries hotel, I took a deep breath before I entered through the double front doors to meet my dad and his soon-to-be fiancée (ick) for lunch. I knew it would be slamming salt in my wound to eat there but was I going to deny myself my favorite drink because of a man?

No way.

Sure, Paul had pawned me off on some guy whose name sounded like a board game production company. But what was so horrible, really, about Milton sending a box to my work this morning with a note saying he looked forward to Paul introducing us at the Black & White Ball tonight? It wasn't exactly awful that the box had contained a gorgeous white strapless dress with a black satin sash in exactly my size. Yeah, I'd tried to hate the dress and all it represented of my mother's wicked influence but—I kid you not—when I'd tried it on, I felt like a freaking fairytale princess in that thing. Milton may be extravagant, but he had good taste!

So . . . I'd hold my head high, smile through date number five, and have lunch wherever I wanted—no matter *who* worked there.

As I crossed the marble lobby a magnetic force pulled my eyes toward the concierge desk. No Paul. Instead, an elderly man stood there talking animatedly on the phone. Telling myself I didn't care that he wasn't there, I continued down the hallway. When I started to pass the lounge, my gaze darted to the bar. A blonde woman was pouring wine into several glasses. Again, no sign of Paul. My shoulders heaved in disappointment and I recognized that part of me had come here hoping to see him.

Maybe he wasn't working today because he was working tonight?

Wait, why did I care when he'd rejected me? Get a grip, Kaitlin. It was *good* that Paul wasn't here. Bad enough that I'd have to see him tonight when he introduced me to Milton. I started up the stairs to the restaurant.

"Kaitlin?" a female voice said.

I glanced up and recognized Paul's co-worker coming down the steps. "Hi, um . . . ?"

"Alice." She stared at me as if in shock. "What are you doing here?"

"Meeting my dad for lunch," I said, wondering why she'd be surprised to see me. "Is Paul working today?"

My heart pounded and I wanted to kick myself for asking.

Her forehead wrinkled. "No, he's . . . out."

"Oh." I kept my face blank since I had the distinct feeling she knew where he was and wasn't telling me. Maybe beautiful Alice was the reason he'd passed me off to his friend. But that didn't make sense either because he'd kissed me and I'd believed him when he'd said he preferred committed relationships. Although, I'd believed a lot of things in my life that hadn't come true. "Well, nice to see you again, Alice."

"Have a great lunch," she said, in a tone that didn't exactly scream jealousy.

"Thanks." I flattened my lips, feeling like Paul had once again disappointed me, then I shook my head. I had enough problems to deal with. Namely, at the top of the stairs.

My dad stood in the waiting area wearing a navy-blue suit and his peppered hair was feathered back in the same style he'd worn since I was a little girl. He was bouncing on his heels next to a middle-aged brunette with a bobbed cut who was talking to the hostess.

"Hi, Dad."

He turned around, looking nervous like a school boy about to ask a girl to prom. "Kaitlin." He stepped toward me, leaned forward too quickly and bonked his forehead into mine. "Sorry, honey. Are you all right?"

With my hand on my forehead, I stared up at my normally calm, cool, and collected dad. "I'm fine. Don't worry."

"If you're sure." He moved slower this time and gave me a kiss on the cheek. "Honey, this is Jennifer."

I held out my hand. "Hi, Jennif—"

"I'm so happy to meet you!" She pulled me into a crushing hug. "Your dad talks about you non-stop. He's so proud. Congratulations on your new home. I can't wait to hear all about it."

Whoa. Not at all formal and reserved like I was used to. No, Jennifer was not what I'd anticipated with her warm and bubbly personality. I mean, she didn't even sound like she was trying to steal my dad from me.

My head spun as she released me. "Um, thank you."

The hostess showed us to our seats where I promptly ordered a Geoffries Martini. To my surprise, Jennifer ordered the same saying that this was my town and therefore I must know what was good. The constant chatter was a bit overwhelming but the more we talked, the harder I was finding it not to like her.

When we were just about finished with lunch, Jennifer excused herself to the restroom.

My dad set his fork down and dabbed his mouth with his napkin. "What do you think, honey? I'd love your approval before I propose."

"Well, she. . ." I fought for any reason I could find for my dad not to marry her, but I couldn't think of a single one. "Honestly?"

His hopeful expression froze. "Please."

My eyes watered. "She's wonderful. Of course you have my approval."

Dad's eyes got misty. "I'm sorry, honey. I know I blew it the first time around with your mom. I just couldn't make her happy."

I scoffed. "Nobody can."

His brows came together. "From what you've told me over the years, she and Gary seem to do all right."

That's because my stepdad's adoration for my mom made him oblivious to all of her shortcomings. Huh. "You're right. They do make each other happy."

"See? Things can work even better the second time around." Dad's voice quavered. "How is your love life? You must've had a rough time with the wedding called off last spring."

My eyes widened in shock. My dad had never delved into my personal life. Ever.

Jennifer picked that moment to return to the table.

"What did I miss?"

I turned toward her vivacious expression, wondering if her open personality had rubbed off on my dad. "Well, I—"

"Kaitlin," came a familiar male voice.

Chills vibrated through me. Swallowing, I looked up into blue eyes and an unexpected rush of heat ignited my belly and curled my toes. "Paul? I thought you weren't working today."

"I'm technically not." His dark-tousled hair appeared wet from a shower as he stood there in dark jeans and a short-sleeved button-up shirt. He looked amazing, as usual. Except. . . .

My eyes narrowed on a blue smudge just below his ear. "You have paint or something by your jaw."

"Thanks." He rubbed his fingers over where I'd pointed then turned to my dad and Jennifer. "How's your lunch? Is there anything more I can get for you all?"

"Oh, sorry." I'd been so surprised (and excited) to see him, I'd forgotten my manners. "Paul works for the hotel. Paul this is my dad and his girlfriend Jennifer. They flew down from Seattle."

Paul held my dad's eyes as he shook his hand. "How

long are you in town, sir?"

"Call me John." Dad gave him a firm handshake then slipped his arm around Jennifer. "I'm here on business today, with just enough spare time to meet my little girl for lunch."

"It's nice to meet you, Paul." Jennifer smiled and my eyes bulged when she popped up and gave him a quick hug. "How did you and Kaitlin meet?"

Jennifer's question didn't seem to have any hidden motivations other than general curiosity. Interesting to note how different she was from my mom.

"We met here at the hotel, actually." Paul gave me a side-glance and the dimple in his cheek deepened. "I was tending bar and she ordered a Geoffries Martini."

Jennifer held her glass up. "Thanks to Kaitlin, I've had my first one. They're delicious."

Paul's smile deepened. "Thanks to Kaitlin, I rappelled down my first building with her this week."

Dad turned toward me with raised brows. "You did that, honey?"

I bit my bottom lip. "It was spur of the moment."

Just like our kiss had been. . . .

"It sounds like you bring out my daughter's

adventurous side, Paul." The sides of my dad's eyes crinkled as he smiled. "And here I thought Kaitlin had ignored my calls all week because she was at home remodeling her house."

My cheeks heated. "I meant to call you back, Dad."

"Have you seen the house yet?" Paul said, seeming anxious for an answer.

The waitress came by, eyed Paul curiously, then quietly left the bill on the table.

"Unfortunately, no." Dad shook his head and reached for the bill. "We'll have to make another trip down for that."

Paul lifted the bill, slipped it into his pocket, then nodded to my dad. "I'll take care of this for you—perk of working for a hotel. Very nice meeting you and hope you enjoy the rest of your day."

Jennifer and Dad turned to me since I'd pretty much been mute.

I cleared my throat. "Thanks, Paul. I guess I'll, um, see you tonight."

"Definitely." With a final nod, he left.

A knot formed in my belly. It had seemed so natural with Paul here that I'd almost forgotten his rejection.

"He *likes* you." Jennifer's voice held a teasing tone. "Are you two dating?"

I shook my head. "He's just a friend."

"Seems like more than that." She smiled knowingly. "Have you told him how you feel? It's written all over your face."

Worse, I'd asked him out. "Trust me, it's not like that between us."

She put a hand on my arm. "He's into you, trust *me*. Isn't that right, John?"

Dad looked from Jennifer to me. "Tell him how you feel, honey. Don't wait as long as it took your old man to figure things out. If you want something, you have to go for it."

"Oh, really?" I laughed, wondering when I'd get used to my dad being so forward with his thoughts. Such a new venture for us. But maybe some things really were better the second time around. Sure seemed like it for my parents and for Kristen, too.

If only it could be that way for me.

****

After making the driver wait for half an hour, I finally climbed into the limo that Milton had sent to take me to the Geoffries hotel for date number five. Yeah, this was the first time I'd been late in my life but I couldn't stop thinking about Paul. Finally, I'd convinced myself I needed to be rational, hold my head high, and reach my goal. Five dates in five days and this was the last one.

My stomach roiled like I was making a huge mistake.

Why had Paul showed up at the restaurant to meet my dad? I couldn't figure him out. Obviously Alice had told him she'd seen me there. But why would she do that? Both Jennifer and my dad thought Paul liked me but I'd asked him out and he'd said no. I'd put myself out there and he'd rejected me flat. Then he'd kick-punted me to his friend as if my mom's type of guy was what I wanted, which wasn't true.

I wanted Paul, but he didn't want *me*.

Wind chimes tingled and I reached into my black satin evening bag for my cell. I checked the screen which showed an incoming call from Ellen. "Hello?"

"Is everything all right?" Her voice squeaked as if she were worried. "Are you on your way to the Black & White Ball?"

Unfortunately. "Yes. Why?"

"Oh . . . no reason. Just checking. Aren't you

supposed to be there at eight?"

I stared at my phone then put it back to my ear. "Since when do you monitor my dates?"

"Pfft. I don't." She gave a small laugh as if the suggestion were ridiculous. "I'm actually calling to thank you for your advice."

I blinked. "What advice?"

"About the sex of the baby, silly. Hang on."

I heard chatter in the background and a familiar female voice. "Where are you? Is that Ginger?"

"Sorry about that." Her voice came out rushed. "Yes, that's Ginger. We're out and she said hi."

"Hi, back." I peeked through the rear window at the city lights as we rolled into downtown Sac. "So you talked to Henry about finding out the sex of the baby? And?"

"I told Henry how I felt and he said he had no idea it meant that much to me and of course we could find out the baby's gender." She laughed. "Can you believe that?"

Hearing the joy in my friend's voice made me smile. "I'm happy for you, Ellen."

"Thanks." She lowered her voice. "So crazy that I spent all that time thinking he knew how I felt. Men can be so clueless. I have to go. Have a great date!"

"Bye." I put my phone back in my purse as Ellen's words echoed in my head.

Men can be so clueless.

Was it possible my dad and Jennifer were right and Paul had no idea I was in love with him? Wait . . . in *love*? No way. I mean, sure, I had strong feelings for him and, yeah, I melted whenever he touched me . . . but *love*?

Oh, no.

I picked up the phone to ring the driver. "Can you pull over to the curb right here, please?"

As soon as we stopped, I burst out of the limo and paced in front of some dance club. The loud music thrummed through the wall making my ears pound. Or maybe my ears were pounding because I'd just realized I was in love with Paul and had the first fleeting hope that he might love me back.

The limo driver stepped into my path. "Miss? Is everything all right?"

"No!" For once in my life I would not pretend everything was all right. "I'm in love with someone but I'm going on a date with another guy."

The short and stocky driver furrowed his bushy brows. "Why don't you just go out with the guy you're in love with?"

I stared at this total stranger who made perfect sense. "Because I asked him out and he said no even though he rappelled down a building with me, opened up to me about his family, and kissed me like he never wanted to stop."

He held his hand up. "Why did he say no then?"

There was the million dollar question. I threw my hands out. "I have no idea."

He rubbed his chin. "Did you ask him?"

I stopped pacing and blinked. "No."

He shrugged. "Well, then. Maybe you should?"

"You're right." I swallowed the mass of fear creeping up my throat. "I'll do it. Let's stay parked at the curb while I call."

The driver opened the door for me, which seemed overly formal considering I'd just spilled my guts to him but I thanked him anyway. Then I pulled out my phone, found the familiar Southern California phone number, and dialed. My heart pounded in my chest but after four rings it went to voicemail: *This is Paul. Leave a message.*

A loud *beep* sounded in my ear. "It's Kaitlin. I need to talk to you and it's pretty urgent. Call me when you get this please."

Adrenaline coursed through my veins and every second I waited for him to phone back felt like a thousand years. I should have opened up to him about how I felt a long time ago. Why hadn't I? I'd been so focused on keeping it together and pretending his rejection was all right. Why?

My eyes narrowed and I punched my mom's phone number.

She answered on the second ring and without the usual formalities. "I was hoping you wouldn't call me until I'd calmed down."

Until *she'd* calmed down? "What are you talking about?"

"You must know I've spoken with Alisha." She *tsk tsked* into the phone like I was ten and hadn't cleaned my room. "I've been trying to undo the damage you caused last night, but I'm afraid Brian is under the impression you're not interested in him."

My jaw tightened. "That's because I'm *not*. I'm not going to waste his time when I'm in love with Paul."

"The bartender?" She gasped. "You're not thinking clearly, honey. I know canceling the wedding was upsetting, for all of us, but you're not a teenager and can't rebel like this."

I guffawed. "When did I ever rebel as a teenager?"

"Need I bring up how you chose U.C. Berkeley over Stanford? I thought daddy would have to pick out my casket."

"Cal is a *great* school!" I retorted, then realized we'd gotten slightly off track. "Mom, I'm done pretending anymore. Calling off the wedding was awful but I'm glad it happened. Besides the cheating part, he wasn't right for me. I couldn't open up to him and be myself the way I can with Paul."

Silence.

"Paul is sweet and thoughtful and he makes me happy." A huge weight lifted as I confessed everything to my mom. Like I'd been freed from chains and could just be myself now whether she liked it or not. "He's a great bartender and a hard worker. He even fills in for staff members on their days off. Plus he moved to Sacramento to be close to his mom when his dad passed away. How sweet is that?"

Long pause. "Well, I could never approve of someone who wasn't kind to his mother."

I shook my head. "Did you say approve?"

She sighed. "I can't say I understand your choices but I survived Berkeley, didn't I?"

A burst of laughter escaped. "Thanks, Mom."

When I hung up the phone, it suddenly seemed twice as urgent to tell Paul how I felt about him. I dialed his number.

This is Paul. Leave a message.

The *beep* went off in my ear. "It's me again. I can't meet your friend Milton. I'm sorry. Please call me."

Oh, man. I'd just blown date number five. All bets were off the table now. I was going for it with Paul and nothing was going to stop me. I racked my brain trying to figure out why he wouldn't answer his cell when I knew he was at work. Duh. He was at *work*. I pulled up a search engine on my phone, got the number for the Geoffries hotel, and tapped them into my keypad.

My hands shook as I held the phone to my ear and I knew I'd never been this nervous in my life. "Hi, I'd like to speak with Paul. He's one of your employees and it's really important."

"I'm sorry, we don't have a Paul who works here," the man said.

I rolled my eyes. "Yes, you do. I've seen him there numerous times. He's the bartender."

"Ma'am, we don't have a bartender named Paul."

I gripped my phone. "Then how did he serve me drinks Monday night in *your* lounge? And why did I see him Wednesday night covering for Manuel at the concierge desk?"

Don't ask me how I remembered Manuel. I'm totally bad with names.

The man paused a moment and I heard him speaking to someone in the background. "Oh, I apologize. I didn't realize you meant Paul Geoffries. I was just told he filled in for Manuel Wednesday night."

Geoffries? What the . . . ?

My mouth fell open. "Did you just say Paul *Geoffries*?"

"Yes, ma'am. He's making a speech right now at our Black & White Ball, but I can take a message for him if you'd like."

My face went numb. "No, thanks."

I pressed the END button then dropped my hands

onto my lap and stared at my white satin dress that was glowing in the darkness of the limo. There must be some mistake. My Paul couldn't be Paul Geoffries because that would mean he owned the hotel. Not possible. He was too young and the Geoffries hotels have been around forever. . . .

Although Paul's father had recently passed away. No, this was crazy. I pulled up a search engine just to prove how silly the concept was and that the front desk person had to be wrong. When the prompt pulled up, I typed in: *Paul Geoffries, hotel, Sacramento, CA.*

I clicked on the first article, which was from the *Sacramento Social Scene* website.

Triple S has great news for all the single ladies in our fair town—bad boy Paul Geoffries is back on the Sacramento Social Scene. After hot hook-ups this year with Tiffany Heart, lead singer of Street Knights, and Hollywood glamazon, Virna DiAngelo, this trust fund bachelor is back on the prowl. So have fun ladies, be safe, but hold onto your hearts as this bad boy isn't likely to settle down any time soon!

Stunned, I paused for a minute then searched: *Paul Geoffries, Hollywood.*

Clicking on the first article, I read: *After a high-profile break-up with actress Virna DiAngelo, it's more tears for bad boy Paul Geoffries. We've just learned that hotel magnate, Milton P. Geoffries Senior, died peacefully in his Granite Bay home Saturday night with his wife, Irene Geoffries, by his side. The hotel chain is still privately owned, which means Mr. Geoffries' billion-dollar business will now be run by his wife and son. Funeral arrangements have yet to be announced and the family is requesting that the media respect their privacy during this difficult time.*

Tears burned my eyes as I thought about how crushed Paul had been by his dad's passing. Moments later I realized that Milton P. Geoffries *Senior* meant that there had to be a Milton P. Geoffries *Junior*. Paul had set up my date number five with himself? Why? It had to be part of his elaborate scheme. Some kind of joke. . . .

That bad boy had played me like a fool, getting his kicks off making me believe he was a bartender and acting like his discount on patio tiles was some big thing. Money was nothing to him. He was rolling in it and my poor budget must've given him a great laugh.

I'd been deceived. Again. But this time hurt a

thousand times worse.

Wind chimes tingled and my cell lit up with that Southern California phone number. That *Hollywood* phone number. Anger coursed through me and I pressed ANSWER then held the phone to my ear. "Hello, Milton."

Pause. "Are you here, Kaitlin? I'm heading outside."

I noted the strain in his normally confident tone. "Don't bother. I'm not there and I'm not coming."

"Sweetheart, let me explain. . ."

My eyes narrowed at that term of endearment. "Congratulations on winning your game. You completely fooled me. What's the fun for next week? Making some naive woman believe you're the front desk clerk?"

"Kaitlin, I—"

"Save it, Milton." My jaw quivered as hot tears escaped down my cheeks. "I don't want to hear another word from your lying mouth ever again."

Call Ended.

My throat tightened and my chest ached like a balloon about to explode. Gasping, I grabbed a napkin and crumpled my face into it. Shoulders shaking, I fought to control my sobs, to make it appear that everything was all right like I used to be able to do—but the sobs rippled out one after another with no end in sight.

Chapter Ten

I'd been played. Big time. I threw myself down on my couch, yanked a throw pillow into my lap, and squeezed the soft cushion senseless as I stared at the ceiling. Why had Paul come into my life and toyed with me like that? And what was with him hanging with me all week long? He had everything. He'd even dated Virna DiAngelo! I gave a pathetic laugh, remembering how I'd immediately dismissed her as his ex. Yeah, the joke had definitely been on me.

My doorbell chimed an old-fashioned *ding dong* and I peeked between the window blinds and saw a silver truck parked at the curb. I pushed to my feet slowly, then peered through the keyhole. Frowning, I pulled open the door.

Paul stood on my front porch looking so unbelievably handsome in his black tux and white tie that he took my breath away. His dark tousled hair made his electric blue eyes stand out and I was reminded of my vision of him coming toward me in a tux. My forehead creased. But I'd envisioned Paul. Not Milton Geoffries.

Putting a hand on my hip, I said, "Isn't it considered rude for the host to leave his own ball?"

He reached for me. "Kaitlin. . ."

I immediately stepped back. "Please leave."

"Not until you hear me out." Unfortunately, the wide space gave him the perfect opportunity to push past me and he shut the door pinning me against it. He cupped my face in his hands. "I was going to tell you everything tonight."

Gazing up into his eyes made me want to melt against him. "I don't believe you."

He ran his thumbs over my cheeks. "I never lied to you about who I was."

Twisting away from him, I scoffed. "Okay, Milton."

"The name is part of who I am, yes. But I go by Paul." His eyes peered into mine. "I'm the same person you met. Nothing's changed."

I stared at him incredulously. "I thought you were a bartender."

He started to take a step toward me until my frown deepened, then he slipped his hands into his pockets and stopped. "I'm a bartender, the concierge, and every other job that comes with having a hotel chain. My dad started the Geoffries from the ground up. When he left it to me, I knew I wanted to follow in his footsteps. I work every position to learn the business from the inside out."

That sounded so . . . practical. Not to mention down to earth. Especially for a Hollywood bad boy. "You hooked up with Tiffany Heart from Street Knights."

He shook his head. "An absolute rumor. She's a friend from my college days at U.C. Santa Barbara, but we've never been together."

I tilted my head. "You did date Virna DiAngelo, though."

He held his hand up. "I told you about Virna."

I crossed my arms. "She's not just any ex. She's a movie star."

"I enjoyed the L.A. scene for awhile." He ran his hand through his hair. "Then my dad got sick and I realized what was important in life. Virna's a wonderful person, but I didn't want to spend my life with her."

My head spun. "Every guy wants to spend his life with Virna. She's gorgeous."

His brows came together. "You think that's all I need?"

I shrugged. "I obviously wasn't good enough for you.

You turned me down."

"I turned you down for date number four." His stance shifted then he stepped toward me slowly as if gauging my reaction. When I didn't retreat, he came even closer until we stood just a foot apart. "Kaitlin, I want to be with you. I set myself up as date number five because I plan to be the last date you ever have."

Butterflies danced in my belly, but I pressed my fingers to my temples and shook my head. "I don't know what to believe."

He closed the distance between us and tucked a loose piece of hair behind my ear. "Just before my dad died, he told me he was going to leave me his legacy. When I thought he meant the hotel chain, he chuckled."

I imagined the same chuckle I'd heard Paul make so many times and wondered if Milton had the same blue eyes.

"He told me he meant my mom—that she was the greatest wealth of his life." He fingered the long red strands resting on my shoulder. "That's when I realized what was important. It's not living on the Hollywood circuit or attending exclusive parties. It's about finding a connection with someone and holding onto it until your very last breath."

My eyes widened as I stared up into those sapphire blues that had darkened, deep and intense. I wanted so badly to believe him, but I'd been promised the world before. "Those are beautiful words, Paul. But I've read a lot of words about you today and many of them included the words 'bad boy.'"

He tilted his head and gave me a side-glance. "Are you talking about the tabloids?"

I put my palm to my forehead. "The article said—"

"They're not interested in the truth, Kaitlin—just selling as many of their rags as possible in any way they can." He lifted my hands. "You *know* that. You know *me.*"

Hotel chains. Private jets. Movie stars. This was definitely *not* the Paul I knew.

My hands tingled where he held them, but I shook my head. "I don't know you. I thought I did, but then I found out you're someone else."

A pained expression crossed his face. "I've opened up to you more than I have to anyone, Kaitlin. That's all I can do."

"It's not enough." My chest ached as I finally realized

the truth. This man in front of me was not who he had appeared to be. He'd deceived me. "I've done what you asked and heard you out. Now, please go."

Those blue eyes pierced mine and seemed to plead with me until I finally turned away. Then I heard his footsteps as they crossed the floor, the door squeaked open slowly, and it clicked shut.

Biting my lip, I swung around and stared at the back of the door. Paul was gone. Or Milton. Or whoever he was. My chest went hollow, pain sliced my gut, and it felt like the scars he'd left behind would never heal.

I told myself I'd been *fine* on my own before and I would be again. Only, it didn't feel that way. I glanced toward my kitchen at the half-empty bottle of wine and before I knew it I was pouring myself a glass. I needed to go to my happy place and needed to make it mine again.

As I passed the wall in the kitchen where Kristen had ripped off that rooster wallpaper, I suddenly realized something. Kristen's call from the Geoffries about an opening for her ballroom wedding six weeks from now had been no coincidence. Paul had arranged it.

My heart melted a little, but I took a deep breath and reminded myself that was just money. And Milton was rolling in it.

Holding my wine glass, I slipped open the living room slider, and my heels sank into the lawn as I crossed my backyard. As I walked, Paul's words echoed through my head and I wanted to believe them. Especially the part about finding the connection between us, because I felt it too. But words were easy to come by. So were limos and fancy white dresses when you had more money than you'd ever need.

My eyes burned and the railroad-tie steps blurred in front of me, and I thought about turning back. My heart told me that Paul's words were the truth, but my head told me I'd been burned before. A war waged inside me between what I knew in my heart and what I feared with my head. Then at the bottom of the steps, I looked up and froze.

I stared wide-eyed at my happy place, a tear spilling down my cheek as chills vibrated through me. Instead of dead grass and dirt, a patio of terra-cotta tiles splayed out before me. My heels clicked against the tiles as I stepped forward, gaping in awe. The Adirondack chairs and beverage table had been stained the perfect shade of blue, reminding me of the ocean in Kauai. In addition to all I'd planned, there was also a border running around the patio with bushes of colorful flowers that had a tropical look about them, and through the center lay a tiled pathway to the water.

My first thought was that Paul had hired someone to make my dream come true. But then I remembered lunch with my dad. Paul had showed up last minute, freshly showered, and with paint smeared on the side of his jaw. *Blue* paint.

Paul had done this himself. For me.

A twig snapped behind me and a *crack* echoed across the quiet night. I spun around, then nearly spilled my wine because there he stood on the first railroad tie. I wanted to say something, throw my arms around him, but I felt too stunned to do anything but blink through watery eyes. I watched him approach me.

"I lied to you earlier." He dropped off the last railroad-tie and came toward me in sure and steady steps. "I told you there was nothing more I could do to convince you."

I lifted my lashes as he closed the space between us. "Paul?"

"Kaitlin." He set my wine glass down, cupped my

face in his warm hands, and tilted my face toward his. He peered into my eyes with his deep blues. "I love you."

Tingles danced across my chest and down my arms. I stretched onto my toes, gazed into those ethereal eyes, then paused a breath away from his lips. "I love you, too."

As if that was all he needed to hear, his mouth captured mine and my world exploded into a dream. The rippling water echoed behind me as Paul kissed me sure and strong like he wanted to claim me. But I was already his. Our mouths opened as we explored, tasted, and savored each other. I snaked my arms around his neck, then wove my fingers into that thick tousled hair, wanting to pull him even closer and never let him go.

When he finally leaned back, I was breathless. His arms went around me, his lips curved upward, and he lifted me against him. I threw my head back and laughed as my feet left the ground and he twirled me around and around—pure bliss flowing through every cell in my body.

In this moment, I found my true happy place.

And that was with Paul.

****

Instead of coming to the Black & White Ball in a limo, I arrived in a silver truck, but I'd ended up on a date with Milton after all. My black heels clicked across the marble lobby floor and I gazed over at Paul who slipped his hand into mine and winked at me.

Warmth flooded my belly as we headed down the hall, then strolled into the Geoffries' grand ballroom hand in hand. The waiter at the entrance did a double-take at Paul and me before serving each of us a glass of champagne.

I bit my lip and raised my flute. "To you finally agreeing to go on a date with me."

Paul lifted his glass toward mine. "What do you think we've been doing all week? I've just been waiting for you to realize it."

My mouth spread into a wide grin. "Sneaky guy."

He clinked his glass into mine. "Sweetheart, you haven't seen anything yet."

I sipped the bubbly liquid and surveyed the room. Black and white drapery, an incredible crystal chandelier above us, and elegantly dressed guests scattered across the entire room. A wooden dance floor took up the far corner of the room where hundreds of people were getting down to a hit song I recognized from the radio.

My eyes squinted as I peered at the band. "Oh, my . . . is that the Street Knights?!"

Paul chuckled. "Most definitely. I'll introduce you to the band when they take a break. I think you and Tiffany will hit it off."

"Tiffany Heart and me?" I couldn't imagine what I'd possibly have in common with the Grammy winner. "How exactly did she become a knight, anyway?"

"It's a long story. I'll let her tell you." He laughed, then brushed his lips against my cheek. "Would you like to dance?"

"I'd love to." I followed him across the room toward the pumping music. We reached the edge of the dance floor and as we set our drinks on the table, an enchanting fragrance wafted up my nose and filled me with joy. My eyes flashed to the glass bowl center piece filled with white-petaled flowers that had bursts of yellow at their core. My hand flew against my chest. "Paul, those are plumeria flowers."

The corner of his mouth lifted. "You told me you wanted a white dress, music, plumeria flowers, and your friends."

I followed his gaze to the edge of the dance floor where familiar faces greeted me, smiling. Ellen and Henry. Kristen and Ethan. Ginger. Melanie and Matt.

Ellen waved. "It's about time you got here!"

Placing my hand along the side my mouth, I shouted, "Better date than never!"

Mel gave me a knowing look, nodded her head at Paul, then mouthed, "I told you so."

I nodded, smiling.

The band switched to a slow tempo and Tiffany belted out the beginning of a love song about *saying what you want*, *getting what you want*, and the familiar song had never rung truer. Ginger, Ethan, and Kristen stepped off the dance floor. Ethan shook Paul's hand and they began chatting as I turned to my friends.

Ginger rubbed her hands together. "Looks like you've done it."

Kristen raised her brows. "Are we on for painting tomorrow?"

I shook my head. "I'm afraid not."

Ginger's brows came together. "But the bartender is date number five—"

"No, he's not part of the game." I hugged Ginger first

and then Kristen. "Thank you."

Kristen squeezed me back. "For what?"

My eyes watered as she released me. "I thought by consuming myself with the remodel, I was making my house my sanctuary. In reality, I was hiding. Not wanting to hurt again." I shook my head. "I wouldn't have met Paul if it weren't for you both."

"Glad we could be of service." Ginger laced her arm through Kristen's. "Now we just need to find a man for me. I'm thinking someone like that guy right there. Or maybe him."

I laughed as Ginger pointed from the Street Knight's hot guitarist, to their keyboardist.

"Ladies," Paul came over and held his hand out to me, "mind if I steal her away?"

He led me to the dance floor, twirled me around once—my white satin dress flying around me like a ballerina—and then he pulled me against him.

I lifted my lashes. "You invited all my friends?"

He shrugged. "I sent the tickets to Kristen and she did the rest."

I glanced down at my white strapless gown with its black satin sash. "You picked this dress out for me?"

He grinned mischievously. "Alice helped me out. She's my assistant."

A bright light flashed above my head. "So that's why I always see her with you."

He tapped my nose playfully as we swayed to the music. "I did approve of the dress if that counts for anything."

I grinned. "It counts for a lot. All of it."

His sapphire-blue eyes gazed into mine. "You said you wanted the fairytale ending in a white dress, but I'm giving you a fairytale beginning. For now."

My stomach flipped as the air between us thickened and pulsed—matching the heavy pounding rhythm of my heart. "I lost my bet. You're going to have a lot of painting to help me with."

He brushed his fingers along my cheekbone. "Your wish is my command."

Then he kissed me and I was in my happy place.

Epilogue

Two months later. . . .

News Article: *Sacramento Social Scene*

Photo (man and woman embraced in a kiss as they rappel down a building)

Triple S has discovered that the man in this photo is actually Milton Paul Geoffries Junior, hotel heir and former Hollywood playboy. The woman in the photo has been identified as local Human Resources Manager, Kaitlin Murray. Reports have been circulating that the couple is engaged. Both parties declined to comment, but Triple S was able to get this statement from Geoffries' ex Virna DiAngelo:

Triple S: *Are the engagement rumors true, Ms. DiAngelo? Any idea how the happy couple met?*

Virna DiAngelo: *If I had inside knowledge, I wouldn't be at liberty to say. I would, however, like to formally extend my best to the couple. Paul has been looking for the right woman for a long time and I'm thinking he's finally found her.*

Triple S: *I'm sure Paul and Kaitlin appreciate your*

heartfelt support. Now, please dish on you as we were all thrilled with your Oscar win this year!! What's in the works right now?

Virna DiAngelo: *I've just started work on a new movie. It's about a woman who's given up on love, then she's handed a second chance when the perfect man walks up and serves her a martini. He's not what he seems, but he's everything she never knew she was looking for. It will be released in theatres next year and it's called License to Date.*

The End

SUSAN HATLER is a *New York Times* and *USA Today* Bestselling Author, who writes humorous and emotional contemporary romance and young adult novels. Many of Susan's books have been translated into Spanish and German. A natural optimist, she believes life is amazing, people are fascinating, and imagination is endless. She loves spending time with her characters and hopes you do, too.

You can reach Susan here:

Facebook: facebook.com/authorsusanhatler
Twitter: twitter.com/susanhatler
Website: susanhatler.com
Blog: susanhatler.com/category/susans-blog

Acknowledgments

When I started working on License to Date, I made the decision not to go through the usual drama, trauma, and roller coaster of emotions that occur every time I write a book. This time I'd work in an organized manner and enjoy the smooth, calm process.

Yeah, didn't happen.

I freaked, groaned, pulled at my hair, determined (more than once) that this story was impossible to write and never going to come together. Since multiple people had to endure my mania, I figure a token of gratitude is in order.

Much appreciation to my first readers for their feedback and kind words: Veronica Blade, Tiffany Davis, Virna DePaul, Cyndi Faria, Mike Hatler, Kristin Miller, Ann Rego, and Parisa Zolfaghari. You all rock!

Big hugs to Kristin Miller for being super fun to brainstorm with over coffee and giggles. Smooches to Kate Perry for writing dates with champagne, and for denying me the Internet code at a certain coffee shop when I needed to get some pages written (tough love). Endless hugs and kisses to Veronica Blade, who is always there for me and drops everything when I need her.

Words can never describe how grateful I am for Virna DePaul, who is always the voice of reason during my chaotic writing process, reminding me, "That is exactly what you said the last time."

Most of all, I'm forever thankful to my hubby, Mike Hatler, for listening patiently while I stress (a lot), *bringing me food while I work, giving me shoulder rubs, reading my stories, and for always believing in me. You're my real life romance hero.*

Ellen signs up for online dating because lasting love is all
about compatibility . . .

. . . so why can't she stop
thinking about Henry when he's
the opposite of everything she wants?

Truth or Dare is all fun and games . . .

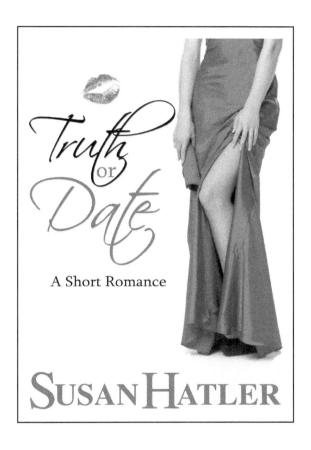

. . . until a spontaneous dare has Gina
falling for the office playboy.

It's Valentine's Day and Rachel can stay home and watch
TV . . .

My *Last* Blind Date

A Short Romance

SUSAN HATLER

. . . or risk another dating disaster
by trying yet again for love.

Kristen swears off men, but temptation
swoops in . . .

Save the
Date
A Short Romance

SUSAN HATLER

. . . when her sexy friend Ethan
starts flirting with her.

Will Melanie have to follow her
best friend's narrow dating rules . . .

A Twist of Date

A Short Romance

SUSAN HATLER

. . . in order to find lasting love?

Kaitlin agrees to five dates in five days . . .

License to Date

A Short Romance

SUSAN HATLER

. . . only to fall for the mysterious bartender
who's there to witness them all.

When Jill's promotion is nabbed by nepotism, she
is offered another position on the partner-track . . .

Driven
to
Date

A *Special* Edition

SUSAN HATLER

. . . by pretending to date Ryan—
the man who got her job.

Holly may be living in her dream location,

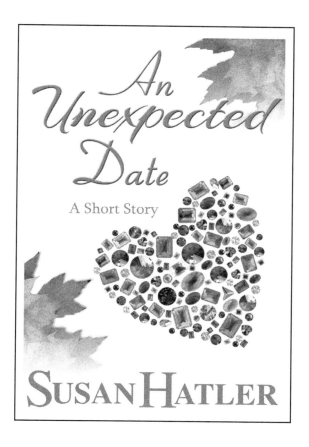

An Unexpected Date

A Short Story

SUSAN HATLER

but is her little resort town too small
to attract the right man?

In high school, it's tough enough reading Steinbeck and
Shakespeare . . .

. . . now Kylie has to read minds.

CPSIA information can be obtained
at www.ICGtesting.com
Printed in the USA
LVHW08s2046170718
584087LV00005B/791/P

9 781499 677195